PRAISE FOR THE STORY OF GOD

"Part Kurt Vonnegut, part Douglas Adams, but let's be honest, Matheson had me at 'Based on the Bible.'"
—Dana Gould, comedian and former writer and producer for *The Simpsons*

"It isn't easy being God, as this book makes quite clear. It's a full-time job and any screwups can haunt you for an eternity. What *Life of Brian* did for Jesus, *The Story of God* may do for the Father . . . or the Son, or the Holy Ghost . . . It humanizes the poor guy, which, after all, is appropriate since he was created in the image of man."
—Lawrence M. Krauss, director of the Origins Project at Arizona State University and author of *The Physics of Star Trek* and *A Universe from Nothing*

"Matheson punctures the pretensions of organized religion with unremitting hilarity."
—Jerry Coyne, author of *Why Evolution Is True* and *Faith versus Fact: Why Science and Religion Are Incompatible*

"Half the people who read this book will laugh out loud, certain Chris Matheson is a twisted comic genius; the other half will laugh silently, equally certain that Chris will spend eternity writhing in hell."
—Ed Solomon, screenwriter of *Men in Black*

"*The Story of God* is an original, funny, and devastating book."
—Jay Phelan, coauthor of *Mean Genes*

D1059022

"If there is a God who wrote the Bible, when he reads this he's going to wonder why his editors didn't point out all the problems in his text before publication. Brilliant and irreverent."

—Michael Shermer, publisher of *Skeptic* magazine, monthly columnist for *Scientific American*, author of *The Moral Arc*

"At times the story Matheson tells of God is not just funny, but laugh out loud funny. It's thought provoking too. I loved it!"

—John W. Loftus, author of *Why I Became an Atheist* and *The Outsider Test for Faith*

"God has never been this damned funny in this pseudo-sacred, sacrilegious piece of silliness. In his debut comic novel, Chris Matheson, screenwriter for the Bill & Ted flicks, grabs a seat at the theater of the absurd for an on-the-scene report about The Story of God. With the Bible as script, Matheson perceives a ready-made fantasy plot, ripe with conflict driven by a divine protagonist. . . . Literalists will cry blasphemy. Thoughtful theists will find more profitable afternoon reading."

—Gary Presley, *Foreword Reviews*

"To say Chris Matheson's *The Story of God* is irreverent would be misleading: irreverent does not begin to cover it. Matheson sets out to be just about as offensive with this treatment of the god of the Bible as is humanly or divinely possible. Whether or not this book proves to be your cup of tea, you have to admire his commitment, not to mention his lack of regard for errant lightning bolts once word of his little book reaches the Almighty."

—David Nilsen, *Fourth & Sycamore*

"This is the version of the bible Gutenberg should have printed. Only difference is, it's much more fun. Hilarious. Irreverent. Timeless."

—Peter Boghossian, author of *A Manual for Creating Atheists*

"Matheson's hilarious romp through the Bible reveals the book for what it is—an Iron Age myth. He also reveals the disdain this myth has for women—they are unclean, portrayed as whores, with daughters sacrificed to God while sons are spared. Why any woman believes in this today is a mystery to me."

—Karen L. Garst, PhD, editor of *Women Beyond Belief* and blogger at www.faithlessfeminist.com

THE STORY OF GOD

THE STORY OF GOD

A Biblical Comedy about Love (and Hate)

Chris Matheson

PITCHSTONE PUBLISHING
Durham, North Carolina

Pitchstone Publishing
Durham, North Carolina
www.pitchstonepublishing.com

Copyright © 2015 by Chris Matheson
Postscript © 2016 by Chris Matheson

First printing in paperback, 2016
ISBN-13: 978-1-63431-077-2

**The Library of Congress has cataloged the hardcover edition as
follows:**

Matheson, Chris.
  The story of God : a biblical comedy about love (and hate) / Chris Matheson.
    pages ; cm
    ISBN 978-1-63431-024-6 (hardcover)
  1. God—Attributes—Fiction. I. Title.
  PS3613.A8262S76 2015
  813'.6—dc23
                                                        2015015018

To S

Based on ~~a true story~~ the Bible

Glossary

Gen.—Genesis
Ex.—Exodus
Lev.—Leviticus
Num.—Numbers
Deut.—Deuteronomy
Josh.—Joshua
Jud.—Judges
1 K.—I Kings
2 K.—II Kings
1 Sam.—I Samuel
2 Sam.—II Samuel
Isa.—Isaiah
Jere.—Jeremiah
Ezek.—Ezekiel
Mal.—Malachi
Hos.—Hosea
Mic.—Micah
Jon.—Jonah
Prov.—Proverbs
Song—Song of Songs
Ecc. - Ecclesiastes
Job—Book Of Job
Mat.—Matthew
Mar.—Mark
Lu.—Luke
Jo.—John
Ac.—Acts
Ephes.—Ephesians
Rom.—Romans
Gal.—Galatians
Esd.—Esdras
Rev.—Revelations
(Thom.—Thomas; apocryphal)

PART I

Chapter One

God sits by himself, alone in the darkness. How long has he been there? It feels like forever. Has it been forever? How did he get here? Who put him here? Did he put himself here? When did he do that? Around him: Nothing. A void, no light. Just him, sitting there in the darkness. Was he sitting? Standing? What was he? Wait . . . Was he even *alone*? What was that sound? Peering down, in the darkness, he realized something.

Underneath him was water; (Gen. 1:2) cold, empty, utterly lifeless. It was creepy. Where had it come from? Did he make it, then forget about it? Did he not make it? And if he didn't—then who did? He had to have made it—yet he couldn't remember doing so. But if he had created water (as of course he had), then why had he created only that much reality and no more? Why had he been sitting there in the darkness, above the water, basically forever? He didn't know why—he just sort of . . . had. But now, for whatever reason, God had a thought: He wanted to *see*.

How would he do it? God tried clapping his hands. Nothing happened. He tried clearing his throat loudly, then closing his eyes tightly and reopening them. Nothing worked. Was he stuck here forever, sitting in the darkness with the lightless water swirling beneath him and absolutely nothing to do? It sounded horrible, "hellish," as he would later say.

God had an idea.

He would speak aloud what he wished for. He had never spoken before. He thought about what he wanted to say. "Light, please?" No, it seemed weak, lacking in gravitas. "Turn on the lights?" Stronger perhaps, but who would he be making this demand of? "I want light." Too childlike.

God sat in the darkness for another chunk of time. How long? He didn't know; time didn't exist yet. Then it hit him. He was sitting slumped, head in hands, listening to the water below, staring at the inky blackness around him through his fingers, when he suddenly knew exactly what to say.

"Let there be light," he called out.

And there was. (Gen. 1:3)

God was delighted. He could do this, he could *make things happen*, create whatever reality he felt like. It was an extraordinary moment for him. An unwanted thought crossed God's mind: "Was someone already there who responded to my command?" Impossible, he was God, he was alone.

"I was obviously talking to myself, commanding myself to make light, that makes perfect sense!" God told himself.

Now that there was light, God could look around. Not much—kind of a big nothingness, in fact. A void, essentially, except for the water below and, well . . . him. He had felt himself before in the darkness, but had never seen himself. Now he did. He had two strong legs, a muscular torso, lean arms. He felt his face—eyes, nose, mouth, ears, hair. Had he made himself this way, "created" himself—or had he somehow always *been* this? He didn't know. If he had created himself, he couldn't remember doing so—but he must have. Because if he hadn't, then who had? It was an unsettling question; he didn't want to think about it.

Another unsettling thing: The penis that dangled between his legs. What was *that* doing there? It was ugly, God thought. There is no way he would have chosen that—it looked monstrous to him. He touched it. It reacted. He scowled and yanked his mighty hand away. This thing was an abomination, he decided. Fascinating in a way perhaps, but bad—stirring certain feelings that seemed somehow . . . wicked. And those hanging, droopy testicles below it? *Hideous.* (God had not discovered his backside yet. When he did, he was not happy.)

Without even speaking, God thought, "I must be covered," and instantly a white robe draped over him, covering his body and hiding the offensive parts. There, that was better. He could move on. He thought for a long time about what to do next, then spoke aloud again. "Let there be sky," he commanded, because as far as he could tell, the water below him was just sort of floating in space and he didn't like that. (Gen. 1:8) Next, God commanded land. He needed to be able to walk around, use his powerful legs, not just sit up in the sky. Land was necessary. And there it was. (Gen. 1:9)

While God was pleased with what was happening, there was a part of him that did wonder why he had waited so long to do this; why he had sat there in the dark for more or less eternity, doing nothing. It seemed stupid now that he realized his own power. "I could have done this all along," he thought. (God was prone to self-criticism, sometimes of a harsh sort. It was a problem that would plague him for a long time to come.)

God was happy to see the dry land, but it looked so bare. There was nothing on it—it was brown and grey and dead silent. Walking around it didn't seem like it would be in the least bit enjoyable. How would he make it better? God had a big idea. "I will make things that are alive," he thought. "Things that will be interesting to watch, that will do things." He began to form an idea of a creature like himself, not only alive, but also conscious—able to think, able to grasp him, know him, *love him.*

But he would start with simple things. "Let there be plants," he commanded. Suddenly the land was dotted with beautiful, fully formed fruit trees. (Gen. 1:12) God looked at them appreciatively. These were very good. Later, in a moment of self-doubt, he would criticize himself for creating trees before he created the sun. But for now, looking at the gorgeous leaves and noble trunks and luscious fruit, God felt proud. "Trees are irresistible," he thought to himself. Which gave him another idea that he filed away; they'd make an excellent test.

God looked down at his creation and smiled. Then his smile slowly faded. Given all his powers, given that whatever he commanded came into being, a bit of dry land and a few trees seemed rather small.

"Let there be *more* lights," God commanded and—well, what can you say? Slowly at first, then faster and faster until it was rather dizzying, the sky began to light up with stars, literally trillions of them—trillions of trillions in fact; there was, in effect, an entire universe. (Gen. 1:14–15) God had not intended to create something this big. A universe a few thousand miles in diameter was what he had been thinking, not this enormous, unwieldy thing. Maybe when he had said, "let there be more lights," he had been too vague. Maybe he should have been more specific—"Let there be one thousand more lights," or something to that effect. But it was too late now. The universe was massive, filled with stars and galaxies and planets. There was probably life sprinkled throughout it, God thought, but quickly realized that didn't matter to him at all. What happened in the rest of the universe was of zero interest to God.

No, he was interested in one world. The earth creatures who would know him and obey him were the main things—the *only* things. He was already thinking of them—how they would love him—how he would test them. (They would fail the test, he'd already decided. That was alright; he was excited about the idea of disciplining them for it.)

So he'd made the universe too big, so what? It was evidence of how powerful he was. Also, he had created the sun and the moon, and he liked them very much. (Gen. 1:16) That damn self-critical voice would pop up in his head later: "Creating the earth and apple trees first and then building the universe around them—good thinking, God." He hated that voice.

Chapter Two

There earth sat, dotted with fruit trees, which now had sunlight to help them grow, which was good. But other than the trees, it was quiet. The trees and the plants didn't do anything. They certainly were not capable of loving him, which was, God now understood, all he really wanted. The plants and the trees were, yes, "alive" . . . but they were so boring. They just sort of sat there, doing nothing.

God decided to fill the water with living, active creatures. He called them "fish." He decided to fill the air with flying creatures he called "birds." (Gen. 1:20) God liked birds at first, but quickly became annoyed with their loud, squawky voices. The smart ones, like crows and parrots, particularly irked him. "*Shut. Up.*" he would find himself thinking as he listened to them chatter. Before long, he would be happy to have all birds killed. God thought the fish were fine; they didn't do anything he disliked. God also created a few sea monsters on this day. (Gen. 1:21)

God made a speech to the birds and the fish, welcoming them to earth and giving them a sense of direction—getting them off to a solid start, basically. He thought about what to say, then decided he'd found the perfect note to strike: "Be fruitful and multiply," he told them. (Gen. 1:22) Which seemed like an excellent message . . . until that damned self-critical voice piped up again: "They're fish and birds, they don't understand you, you do know that, right?" God hated it when he had thoughts like these. They ruined what had been a highly productive day. He had planned on making more living things, but he went to sleep instead. "Also," he lied to himself, "I'm still tired from creating the whole universe yesterday, all those trillions of stars . . ."

God woke up the next day refreshed, ready to continue. "Let there be tiny, creeping things," he commanded, quite pleased with that description of insects. Insects seemed like a splendid idea to God, not least because some of them would be good to eat! (Levit. 11:22) God then created mammals, and he felt very good about them, especially cows, which he instantly knew would taste delicious. (Gen. 1:25) ("I never created reptiles," God later realized, and that bothered him. Who *did* create them? "Why, the same person who created mushrooms and lobsters and crabs and snails and everything else I never mentioned—ME! Who else would have—another god? They don't even exist, so how could they have?")

The stage was set. There was land, water, trees, insects, fish, birds, cows—the whole planet was teeming with life, and that was good, although, you know, utterly pointless. God didn't actually care about any of these creatures, and here's why: Because they didn't care about him! Chimps, elephants, dolphins, wolves—yawn.

It was time to create the creature that would love him. God had been planning this creature, the final and most important one, for awhile now. He would be called "human" and he would look *just like God*! God was thrilled by the idea.

"Let us make man in our image, in our likeness," God heard himself command. (Gen. 1:26) Which was strange. Why had he said that, he quickly wondered. In our image, in our likeness? What did that mean? "Am I so pompous that I refer to myself as 'us,'" he wondered. Or did he, on some level, think that he wasn't alone? That there were other gods up in the sky with him? This thought bothered God a lot. He didn't want there to be other gods; it made him mad to think there were. Because what if there were and the humans, his special creatures, somehow, perversely, ended up liking those other gods more than they liked him? (Which was exactly what would happen, God already knew in his heart.)

Maybe it was a slip of the tongue, God thought. Maybe he'd meant to say "in my image, in my likeness," and had said "in our image, in our likeness" by accident. That could happen to anyone. He wasn't going to worry about it, he told himself. (In truth, he worried about it constantly.)

Just as God would create man in his own image, he would also create the man's companion—"woman," he called her—in his image. Or, you know, sort of. Not exactly, obviously— God wasn't a "woman," but he would create her in his likeness . . . except for the fact that she was, you know, female. ("What are you, some sort of she-male?" Satan would ask him much later, when they were about to fight over the final destiny of humankind, but that is jumping ahead. Anyway. No, God was not a "she-male." He made woman in his own image, but he was all man, what was strange about *that*?)

God hesitated. Why did he even need women? Why couldn't there just be males? Why couldn't they give birth out their anuses? No . . . No . . . It wouldn't work; women were, sadly, necessary. With regard to woman's creation, God considered two options. One was to basically make her at the exact same time as the man. That seemed like a good idea; God decided to do that. Then he decided that he'd make the man first and create the woman from the man's rib. Then he decided that he'd do both. "Can I do that?" he wondered, then instantly rejoindered with "I can do anything, I'm GOD, I can make the man first and *also* create them at the same time!! Watch me!!" So he did—but it was a little bit confusing. (Gen. 1:27 vs. 2:7) (The two "extra" humans that God made he put in cages, where they lived for awhile, then died when he forgot to feed them.)

The man God named Adam. The woman he didn't give a name to, he just called her "woman." (Gen. 3:20) She was certainly attractive; the man obviously thought so, his penis made that obvious. God did not like the way that looked.

"The first chance I get, I'm going to make them cover up," he thought to himself. "Their nudity really bothers me." But for now, he'd let them be naked. It was distracting, though. In the days since discovering his own testicles, God had had a change of heart. He couldn't help but notice what attractive balls Adam had—"perfect" was the word that came to mind. Adam's penis was very nice looking too, though something wasn't quite right. It definitely needed a change. After thinking about it for a while, God decided the man's penis could use one important fix. If the skin at the head of it was trimmed away, it would look even better. Good idea, God thought to himself.

God honestly couldn't grasp what exactly Adam found so alluring about the woman. Not only was she less interesting to God ("My story will revolve around men," he murmured to himself), he also sensed something . . . what? . . . bad about her. Something strange and hidden and disruptive. He didn't *trust* her. He'd just made her and already he wondered if he'd made a mistake. "She's going to create problems," he thought. "She's trouble, I can feel it."

Still, it was with an amazing feeling of pride and accomplishment that God looked down upon his glorious creation. "This is very good," he said to himself. (Gen. 1:31)

And yet . . .

Those damned dark thoughts always seemed to creep in. Where did they *come* from? He had no idea. He'd have eliminated them if he could—but he couldn't seem to. "It's a perfect creation and my two humans, Adam and woman, will be happy and content within it, as I wish them to be. They will live within their beautiful garden forever and they will love me and that will be wonderful," God told himself.

But he knew it wasn't true.

Chapter Three

What was it, God later wondered?

Was it insecurity that made him test them, a fear that they wouldn't obey him? Or was it something else, something even darker? He said he wanted these two to be perfectly happy in the garden he'd made for them, but when he really thought about it—it sounded boring. Perfect happiness forever? What's interesting about *that*?

Especially when there was another way of looking at things. "What if I test them—they will fail, I already know that, obviously—then punish them for that failure by sending them out into the world, which before long they will fill up with more humans, lots more? (These creatures will love sex, no matter how wicked I will tell them it is, and I will tell them that constantly, but it will not matter.) All of these new humans will then also do bad things that I can punish them for, then forgive them for, then punish them for again!" Just the thought of this future sounded very appealing to God. So much to do. God knew himself well enough already to understand that he *loved* drama. Animals were fine. But he found nothing exciting about bears or robins or spiders; they were mainly here to be eaten. God was so uninterested in animals, in fact, that he didn't even name them: He allowed Adam to do it instead, to call them whatever he wanted to. (Gen. 2:19) "I'm surprised there weren't more creatures called 'blaaahhs' and 'urrgghhs,'" God chuckled to himself and—wait—did Adam name himself? (Gen. 2:20)

For the first time, God called on Satan, whom he had apparently created at the same time he created reptiles. From the first, God didn't like the way Satan looked at him. There was something knowing in his eyes. He acted as if he was God's equal, which was ludicrous. "He knows nothing, he is my employee, I created him to work for me and that is all," God thought.

"I want you to enter into my Garden of Eden and trick the woman," he announced to Satan.

Satan studied God silently for a moment, then asked, "Why?"

"It's a test obviously, Satan. I want to see if my humans will obey me."

"You don't know if they will?"

"Of course I know if they will. They won't. Which is exactly my plan."

"Your plan is for them not to obey you?"

Satan's "innocent" questions irritated God. "Exactly!" he snapped.

"But if you already know they won't obey you, then what's the point of testing them?"

God stared at Satan for a second, then shook his head briskly. "Leave the big thinking to me, alright, Satan?" That blank look again. "He's mocking me," God thought. "I should kill him right now. Why do I need this guy? I don't. Creating him, which I obviously did, was a mistake and I'm going to rectify that mistake right now." God glowered at Satan and prepared to kill him— then hesitated, reconsidered. "No. I am God. I do not *make* mistakes. I am, by my own definition, perfect, not even capable of a 'mistake.' Therefore, I must have created Satan for a perfect reason. I will ignore his ridiculous questions and make him do my bidding."

"Here's the point, Satan: I have commanded them not to eat of the tree of knowledge of good and evil." (Gen 2:17)

"The what?"

"The tree of knowledge of good and evil," God repeated, puffing up a bit, quite proud of the name he'd given the tree. "Not pretentious in the least," he'd congratulated himself.

"What is that?"

"It's a tree that contains knowledge of good and evil, obviously."

"And you don't want them to know the difference between them?"

God tightened. He'd had enough of this asinine line of questioning; this wasn't about the damned tree, this was about obedience! "Just listen to what I am telling you to do, alright, Satan?"

Satan crossed his arms and looked at God silently.

"As I said, I want you to test the humans, especially the woman. There is something about her that I don't trust."

"That's because you like men."

God glared at Satan, knowing very well what he meant. "Rise above it, Lord," he told himself. "You are better than this, do not get pulled down to his demonic level."

"As I was *saying*, Satan, I want you to take the form of a talking creature of some sort."

"How about a reptile?"

"A reptile, hmmm—yes, that could work. You will be a talking reptile and you will trick the woman into eating the fruit of the tree of knowledge."

"How should I trick her?"

"Tell her . . . tell her that she will not die if she eats the fruit, ha!" (Gen. 3:4)

"Which is true."

"Which is true, exactly, yes!"

"Even though you already told the man that if they ate the fruit they *would* die?"

"I was setting up the trick, Satan," God explained, as if speaking to a young child, even rolling his eyes a little to imply "how dim you are." Satan just looked back at him.

"You are telling her the truth as part of the trick, do you not understand me, Satan?"

"I do understand you."

That remark hung in the air for a moment. "Oh no you do not," God thought to himself. Satan left soon after that and God breathed a sigh of relief. What a bad person he was, so nasty and insinuating and always with that vaguely bemused tone to his voice, as if he knew something, which he did not. "Why *did* I create him?" God asked himself. "To work against me? Why would I want that? Why would I want someone to undermine and subvert me at every turn? It makes no sense. Only someone who *hated* themselves would want that. And I don't, obviously. I love myself!" Wait . . . Was it even possible? And this was a hard question to ask, but was it possible that he didn't actually create Satan? That Satan just existed, like God? No, that could not be, because if it was, "then I would be a great fraud, falsely claiming to be the creator of everything! But I AM the creator of everything, not just some vain, fatuous, self-obsessed fool who thinks he runs the world when he doesn't!"

Chapter Four

Things worked out precisely as God wanted them to. (They always did, it was a given, but still . . .) Satan tricked the woman into eating the fruit. She then persuaded the man to eat it too. God knew the woman was bad news, but the man's spinelessness surprised him a little. Adam, dear Adam—what a weakling he turned out to be. He didn't even fight it, he just ate the fruit! (Gen. 3:17) "I made him in my likeness and he has bad character. It makes *no sense.*" God muttered to himself.

For a moment, God thought about starting over completely, going back to square one. But could he go back to the start, wipe all this out and begin again? The universe was massive, could he just erase it? He wasn't sure. He decided it wasn't a good idea anyway. "No," he said to himself. "I will not wipe the whole thing out. I will, instead, work with what is here. I will punish the humans, I will kick them out of the garden, make the man work (wait, hasn't he already been working?) (Gen. 2:15) and make the woman suffer when she gives birth (that'll show her!). "I will also," he thought, "punish reptiles by making women hate them." (Gen. 3:15) ("It wasn't reptiles, per se, it was Satan, possessing a reptile; why should reptiles be punished?" that critical voice asked. But God was getting better and better at ignoring it. Still—the way Satan looked at him from inside that reptile really did bother God. As if he had somehow gotten the better of things; as if God was angry because Satan had snuck in and subverted things, rather than having been—as he had been!—*instructed* to subvert God's plan.)

God walked around the garden, looking for Adam and the woman. (Gen. 3:8) He knew where they were, obviously, but he pretended not to because he wanted to scare them a little. Which he did. (Gen. 3:10) God kicked Adam and Eve (he finally, reluctantly, had allowed Adam to name her) out of the garden, and as they trudged away, looking guilty and ashamed of themselves, God briefly felt sorry for them. He quickly killed some cows, rabbits, and goats, skinned them, and made clothes for his humans. (Gen. 3:21) They *were* bad, but he couldn't help but feel a certain affection for them. "Maybe their children will do better," he thought, then instantly knew: No, they won't, they'll *never* do any better, they are bad and wicked and evil. This plan would never work. "Is my plan for my plan *not* to work?" he whispered to himself. Did that make sense? Why would he want his own plan to fail? "Because you hate yourself and want to punish yourself," came a voice from somewhere deep inside him.

God forced himself to think of other things. He watched Adam and Eve exit the garden and enter the "real world" (which was, in fact, not a lot different from the garden. They acted like it was—but it really wasn't.) As Adam and Eve departed, God spoke aloud. "Now that man has become like one of us," he said, "knowing good and bad, what if he should stretch out his hand and take also from the tree of life and eat and live forever?" (Gen. 3:22) God stopped. Wait, what had he just said? "Become like one of *us*?" There was no us, there was only him, *God*. Why did he keep making slips of the tongue like this? It was strange and troubling; it touched on that dark feeling he'd had from the start that there were others around. No. Ridiculous. He was God, the sole creator of the universe and there was no one else around!

But what about that last question he'd asked: "What if he tries to steal from the tree of life and live forever?" There was a tree of life? God didn't remember planting it. Why would he have planted it? Weren't Adam and Eve going to live forever anyway? Why would they need this "tree of life?" Was it really a tree of life, or was it like the so-called tree of knowledge of good and evil, which, in truth, contained exactly one piece of knowledge: Nudity is shameful. (Gen. 3:11)

The thought of Adam sneaking back into the garden to eat of the tree of life bothered God enough that he decided to station guards around the garden to protect it. These were God's first "angels." They were muscular men with wings, dressed in short white robes, all of them quite handsome and fit. He gave them swords and also placed a fiery sword in the air, hovering over the garden, which looked quite frightening. (Gen. 3:24) If Adam tried to steal from that tree of life, God told the angels, cut his head off.

Adam and Eve quickly had two sons, Cain and Abel. "With MY help!" God noted—not 100% sure how he had helped. (Gen. 4:1) Cain grew up to be a farmer, Abel a sheepherder. The first time they brought God gifts was a day he would never ever forget. For the first time, God smelled grilled meat. It was the most incredible thing he'd ever experienced—that rich, smoky, mouth-watering aroma. God felt gratitude to Abel for introducing him to something so wonderful.

Cain brought him some fruit and vegetables, but God was so captivated by the barbecue smell of Abel's grilled meat that he didn't thank Cain, or even acknowledge his gift. (Gen. 4:5) This was, in hindsight, a bit rude, God supposed. It wouldn't have been all that difficult to say, "Oh, and this fruit is delicious too, thank you, Cain." But then again, he was God so it was not rude, it was perfect!

Cain got upset, so God spoke to him. "Why are you upset?" he asked. (Gen. 4:6) He knew the answer, obviously—he always knew the answer; every question he asked was rhetorical in that sense—but he was certainly not going to apologize for liking barbecue so much. Cain didn't respond, he just looked mad. "Sin crouches at the door, waiting for you," God said to him, then nodded to himself, pleased. (Gen 4:7) Sometimes he said things that surprised him in bad ways (the "us/our/we" misstatements), but sometimes in good ways. "'Sin crouches at the door, waiting for you?' Nice imagery, Lord," he thought to himself.

Cain murdered Abel, exactly as God knew he would. But then—an unforeseen problem arose. There needed to be more children. Cain needed a wife, and there weren't any women on earth except for his mother, Eve, and God thought that was a bad idea. ("His uncle would be his grandson," he murmured disapprovingly to himself.) Could God magically create a new woman to be Cain's companion? Of course he *could* do that, obviously—but he decided not to. What he decided to do instead was to magically create an entire tribe of people on the other side of the river, one of whom would become Cain's wife. (Briefly, God regretted having killed his proto-man and woman. "I could have used her here," he noted wryly.)

God started to make the new tribe of people on the other side of the river, then hesitated. They seemed to already be there. That was peculiar. Had he created them at the start without realizing it? Did he not create them at all? Absurd. Of course he'd made them, he'd made everything. He'd simply forgotten when he made them, that was all. Would he create the entire universe and *not* one group of people? No, obviously not.

Still, this was strange. And when Cain quickly went on to form a city—a *city!*—the strangeness deepened. (Gen. 4:17) Again, the thought "Am I a fraud?" flickered across God's mind for an instant before he dismissed it out of hand. "Of course I am not a fraud, I am GOD."

Chapter Five

Several thousand years passed and they weren't pretty. First, angels started sneaking down to earth and having sex with human women, creating half-human, half-angel babies, which God did *not* approve of. Some of them grew to be absolutely gigantic. (Gen. 6:1–4) Thankfully, most of them had heart problems and quickly died off. But that wasn't the real problem. The real problem was this: Humans were bad. They were wicked and evil and did awful, nasty, lawless things. (Gen. 6:11) ("Wait. Can they be doing 'lawless' things when I haven't given them any 'laws' yet?" crossed God's mind, but he ignored the question.) Also, they lived close to a thousand years, *far* too long. "Eighty years is *plenty*," God muttered to himself.

God decided he'd had enough; he'd given the humans a chance and they had failed (as he knew they would, obviously), and now it was time to wipe them all out. He probably should have killed Adam and Eve and started over back then, he now realized. He'd been a patient, tolerant father for a few thousand years, but that was over. "I'll kill everything," God thought to himself.

But how to do it? He could burn them all up, that would be quick and easy—but it was a little *too* quick, he felt. He wanted the humans to suffer a little for their wickedness. Suddenly, he had an idea. "I will drown them all!" he cried out, a broad smile crossing his face for the first time in a long time. "I will make it rain for forty straight days and nights and they will all slowly drown." (Gen. 6:17) It was a simple, elegant plan and God loved it.

But a problem came to mind: How do you drown fish? Not to mention aquatic birds, reptiles, and mammals? Could he drown everything and then, later on, "electrify" the water and fry all those annoying seals and penguins and octopi? In a way, God realized, he would be giving aquatic creatures a huge amount of free food by killing everything else. Why should dolphins be rewarded for the wickedness of mankind? He didn't like the idea one bit, especially when he reflected on the fact that water had been there from the start. What, was he scared of water, intimidated by it, offering up a massive sacrifice of sorts to the giant sea monsters that he knew lurked in the deep?

Nonsense. That was not it, not at all. He simply liked the idea of drowning everything in the world, watching their panicked faces as the water covered their noses and eyes for the last time. And if sea creatures had to benefit in order for that to happen? Well then, so be it. He didn't like it, but he could live with it.

But what about after? God thought to himself. "After I've drowned everything, then what? Should I create two more humans and start over again? Or am I content with a world where sea otters are the most interesting things?" Definitely not. Otters had no ability to love and obey him; they literally didn't even know he existed. Also, he found them aggravating. "Too saucy and full of themselves!" he growled.

God realized he had to leave a few people alive to restart human life. He had to find one good man, that was all. A man he could trust to carry out this most important mission. A man of great strength and character—a truly *good* man.

After a bit of a search, God found a man named Noah who fit the bill perfectly. Noah's father, Lamesh, had killed a child for bruising him, which God heartily approved of. (Gen. 4:23) Noah and his sons Ham, Shem, and Japheth, along with all their wives—God had no idea what any of the women's names were, nor did he really care (Gen. 7:1); he still didn't much trust or like women—would be the survivors of the flood and relaunch life on earth.

God's plan had gotten off to a rocky start perhaps, but now things were about to get a whole lot better. Yet another benefit of this plan: It would put that annoying meddler Satan to work by giving him *lots* of souls to punish in hell. Or—well, actually, it was called "sheol" at this time, and it wasn't much to talk about, just kind of a grey nothingness—but Satan had recently presented a gorgeous plan, a *magnificent* place of endless punishment for those who did not love God. For now, sheol would have to do, but before long Satan would get a huge influx of souls that he would have to attend to and maybe for once, God thought, "he'll be busy enough to stop irritating me." (A question crossed God's mind: What would happen to the souls of all the animals who died in the flood? Wait—did they even have souls? How could he not know that? "Because I don't care, that's how! Animals don't care about me?—well, guess what? I don't care about them either.")

God began to flood the world, dumping huge amounts of rain as well as unleashing giant underground fountains that he had conveniently set up at the start, apparently for this very moment. (Gen. 7:11) It was a glorious forty days: Watching things drown was wonderfully satisfying and, by the time it was over, God had the clean slate he wanted. (Gen. 7:21–23) All the evil and wickedness of mankind had been wiped out. With Noah, his one good man, he could start over, set things straight.

But dammit . . . it didn't quite work out the way God had planned. Or—it *did*, naturally, it always did. But sometimes his perfect plan—well, it didn't make perfect sense to him.

"Do I not want my plan to work out?" he would briefly wonder, before disregarding that thought. "Of course I want it to work out, but I work in mysterious ways!" That always made God feel better.

Still, it was peculiar. The *one* man who God had handpicked to survive, the one good man on earth, Noah? Well, he turned out to be, to put it bluntly, a drunken asshole. Sure, he was obedient, he never talked back once, he did exactly as he was told. "Is that the only reason I liked him?" God later wondered. "*No*. I also liked that he grilled meat for me as soon as he got off the ark." (Gen. 8:20–21) God liked that so much, in fact, that he promised never to kill everyone on earth again (Gen. 8:21), which was a lot to promise, but damn that grilled meat smelled *so* good. "In case I forget this promise, Noah," God had announced, "I will use rainbows as a reminder to myself." (Gen. 9:13) God dug rainbows. He hadn't "planned" them exactly, they were more a by-product of rain and sunshine—but they were so pretty that they occasionally mesmerized him.

For a moment, sniffing that grilled meat, God considered softening his approach to the humans, dealing with them mainly through rainbows and pleasant breezes and falling stars. "I don't have to be so angry all the time. I can be gentle with them." Men were not to be harmed, God announced (Gen. 9:6)—feeling a little weird saying that, given that he'd just killed all of mankind, but still—it was that kind of moment.

But as soon as the barbecue was over, what did Noah do? He got so drunk that he fell down, which caused his robes to fly up, which then revealed his penis and balls! (Gen. 9:21) That was bad enough—if there was one thing God could no longer abide, it was having to see *that* stuff, especially on a guy who was six hundred years old! That part of the body simply does not age well at all, God thought. But it got worse. When Noah's son Ham accidentally walked in and saw his father laying there, what did this belligerent old jackass Noah do? He came to and started yelling at Ham, and not just, "How dare you look at my penis?!" (which would have been acceptable to God because looking at penises was bad). No, it went way beyond that—the old man shouted that Ham's unborn son would be a slave. (Gen. 9:25) Which was crazy. Ham inadvertently walked in and saw his father's penis and now his unborn son was going to be enslaved for it? God thought about scolding Noah for getting so drunk that he fell down. "Don't drink so much, Noah," he considered saying. "Or if you do, wear undergarments."

But he didn't, because . . . well, he'd already stated that Noah was a good man (Gen. 6:9) and how would it look if he turned on him now? "He wasn't actually a good man, I was wrong." God couldn't say *that*. First of all, he wasn't wrong. Even if his plans sometimes didn't make sense to him, they were still perfect. He *knew* that. No, he would stick with Noah. So what if the only words God ever heard him speak were drunken, belligerent nonsense? Nakedness was a shameful, disgraceful thing. True, Ham had not "meant" to see his father naked, it was probably the last thing he wanted to see—probably, but not definitely. After all, homosexuality had been rampant in the world God had just inundated with water. Maybe Ham was a secret, incestuous homosexual? Could he prove he wasn't?

In time it became crystal clear to God: Ham's son *deserved* slavery.

Chapter Six

But things just kept going wrong. No matter what God did, the same problems kept coming up. Later, he would wonder whether using Noah-the-drunken-asshole to spearhead the re-population of the world had been a mistake. Maybe he should have just drowned *everyone* and walked away from the whole thing. He could always look for life elsewhere in the universe and try to work with it. These humans were impossible creatures.

Before long, pretty much everyone on earth congregated in one place. (Gen. 11:2) They all wanted to work together, to build a great city with a tower at the center of it. God did not like this one bit. He found himself speaking aloud: "Let us go down and confound their speech so they cannot understand each other." (Gen. 11:7) Once again, he stopped. Why did he keep saying "us?" There was no *us*, there was only *him*. God found these slips of the tongue extremely disconcerting. Why did they keep happening? "Maybe I was talking to my angels," God decided. Yes, that was it, he was talking to his angels.

But there was another question: Why didn't God want the humans to join together and build a great city? What was wrong with that? Why did he want to split them all up and make them turn on each other? It took him a minute to understand—but then he suddenly did. "Oh," he exclaimed, "of course. It's because I don't like most humans." (God had actually begun to think that the new tribe he had created to give Cain a wife had been rushed and was a bit shoddy: "Not my best work.") "In fact," God continued, "I only like one tiny group of people that doesn't even technically even exist yet, but soon will! In fact, I will basically only like one man for quite awhile. As for the rest of mankind, I don't care what happens to them." In his heart, God had to admit that the people he didn't like . . . well, they didn't seem to like him much either; in truth, they didn't even seem to believe he existed. There was no way he was going to spend any of his valuable time and energy on those idiots. The one group of people he was going to like, the ones who would love and obey him—he didn't want them mixed with the others. They would be special. They would be his chosen ones. He would protect them at times, punish them when necessary (which would be a lot, as it turns out!)

As for the rest, the ones who didn't love him? To sheol with them! To have created the entire universe and everything in it, including every single human being, and then to not even be believed in? That was infuriating to God. Worse, beyond disbelieving, these idiots had the gall to make up other, *nonexistent* gods! They chose to believe in fictional gods rather than him! "Baal," for instance, was a made-up god that many humans (insanely) chose to believe in. "Baal" was supposedly a "fun, sexy" god—"unlike repressed, rigid *real*-God-me, I suppose!" God fumed.

"Why are humans so weak and foolish and needy that they fall for false gods?" God demanded, before stopping himself, not liking that question very much. If Baal *was* real—which, to repeat, he wasn't—but if he was, God felt that he would have been terribly vain, in love with his own supposed "desirability." God loathed the very idea of Baal's self-love, not to mention his obsession with sex. "Sex sex sex, that's all this made-up prick cares about!" God muttered to himself.

God found himself feeling very angry and upset about this; So much so, in fact, that a series of events, frankly, worrisome ones, occurred. God preferred not to think too much about this series of events, choosing to chalk them up to too much wine. "I was simply not myself," God told himself.

In his heart, however, this disturbing series of events would eat away at him for the next few thousand years.

Chapter Seven

Once again, God needed a man to get things going. He looked all over the one small area of the earth that was interesting to him. (Not only was the rest of the universe boring to God, but 98% of earth was too!) Finally, he found a man named Abram. ("Before long, I will add two letters to his name," God thought to himself. "That's how much I like him!") God spoke to Abram, who then started to travel around, claiming the land that God told him to in the very words God suggested: "God, the creator of the universe, gave us this land, forever." (Gen. 13:15) Astoundingly, some of the other tribes didn't accept this. ("They don't believe in *me*, why would they accept my words?" whispered that awful little critical voice in God's head.)

Abram, his wife, Sarah (who wasn't so bad for a woman, God noted), and their slaves (God had zero problem with slavery, obviously) (Gen. 12:5) went to Egypt, where they tricked Pharaoh, which God got a kick out of. Pharaoh was the most powerful nonbeliever on earth, so toying with him was quite enjoyable. "I want to do a lot more of that down the line," he noted to himself.

Abram also traveled with his nephew Lot, who had a bit of a weird, creepy quality to him, God had to admit. Which is presumably why, when they split up, Lot was drawn to basically the worst place on earth: Sodom. God had tried hard to make it clear to people that he despised homosexuality. It was unnatural, *abhorrent.* He honestly had no idea where it came from, this dark and hateful desire that so many men had to enjoy each other's bodies. It was enough to give God momentary pause. "Did I want so many men to be homosexual, was that my plan? Why *would* it be when I hate homosexuality so much? And yet . . . it must be part of my plan because . . . how could it *not* be? But why would I devise a plan that infuriates me? Is it possible that I didn't have a plan, or that I don't even *now?* That I'm just sort of 'improvising' this whole thing, and not even very well?" Or, he continued, very deep in thought now, "Could I be so self-hating that I would create a reality that I would despise just to punish myself? What would I be punishing myself *for?*"

He stopped, shook his mighty head. This was craziness. Of course he wasn't "punishing" himself, he had no reason to do so. None. His mind drifted back to homosexuality and how much he loathed it. "I want to wipe it out forever," he thought. "I don't want any men who are obsessed with penises and balls to walk the earth *ever again.*"

God had a plan. He would send two male angels to Sodom to check up on what he had heard was happening there. "Don't I already know?" he silently asked himself. Yes, of course he knew, he always knew, he was God, he was all-knowing . . . but still, he wanted *proof positive.* God stopped for a moment, another question occurring to him: "If I *am* all-powerful, as I am, of course, then why do I need angels? Can't I do these things myself?" The answer was quick and obvious in this case: God wanted to see what all those homosexuals in Sodom would do when he sent two good-looking male angels into their town. These angels were seriously handsome, "real homo-bait," God thought to himself with satisfaction.

"I will go down to earth with my two angels, whom I will then send into Sodom. Once they prove what I already know to be true, that the town is infested with homosexuals, I will annihilate both Sodom and Gomorrah! I won't even warn them, nor will I need to see what's happening in Gomorrah. I will simply burn them up. No one will survive!" He smiled to himself, thinking of all those damn penis-loving homosexuals being turned to ashes by his heavenly fire.

A vaguely troubling thought popped into God's mind: What about all the women in Sodom and Gomorrah? Why did *they* deserve to die? Was it their fault that they lived in towns where every male from 2 to 100 was a homosexual? Did they really deserve to be burned up for that? God thought this over for a moment, unhappy with the complication—then nodded decisively. "It is exactly what they deserve, they probably drove the men to homosexuality—they are probably homosexuals too!" God had never thought of female homosexuality before. In truth, he didn't think of female anything that much. Women were hidden, strange, untrustworthy. He didn't like them, quite frankly. But maybe they *were* homosexuals too—they probably were. They absolutely deserved to be burned up.

The one straight man in Sodom was Lot, Abram's nephew, who had settled there awhile back (Gen. 14:12) and made a family with his wife (what was her name? Oh well, it didn't matter). He had two teenage daughters who were, even God had to admit, rather attractive. Lot's wife was an unpleasant woman. God didn't like her. "She's probably a lesbian," God muttered to himself, on-the-spot inventing a word to describe female homosexuals. Lot was constantly being gazed at by the men in town, but he didn't seem to notice. He only seemed to have eyes for his own daughters. Which was fine, God thought. "He's the only straight man in town, why shouldn't his daughters have sex with him?" he asked himself.

Chapter Eight

God and his angels flew down to earth and started walking toward Sodom. "As long as we're here," he said to the angels, "let's stop by and visit Abraham and Sarah." (He had added the two letters to Abram's name a while back.) It had been a while since God had paid Abraham a call. During their last visit, he had promised Abraham the land forever, but had attached a price tag: That piece of skin at the tip of the penis that looked so bad? God wanted it removed. (Gen. 17:10–11) "I killed two birds with one stone," God thought to himself, pleased. "I made them sacrifice to me and also enhanced the look of the penis. Why hide that beautiful mushroom head?"

God looked forward to seeing Abraham again. He didn't even mind the idea of a visit with Sarah. ("I can't believe I know her *name*," God mused. "I never know women's names!") As he and the two angels approached Abraham's tent, God felt a momentary twinge of discomfort: "I didn't tell him we were coming, we're just sort of showing up (Gen. 18:2), isn't that kind of presumptuous?" Abraham, however, instantly put God at ease, bowing down and offering food and drink and foot-bathing. God wasn't sure how to respond to Abraham's generosity. "Thank you, that would be very nice"? "Yes, please"? God decided these were both weak. "*Do it*," he said to Abraham. (Gen. 18:5) "Perfect," he thought, "commanding and strong. Not rude in the least!"

Then something incredible happened. For the first time ever, God actually tasted food. (Gen. 18:8) It was *fantastic*. As good as it had smelled, the reality of grilled veal was immeasurably better. God loved it. So did the angels. (Ten hours later, back in heaven, God would be forced to deal with the inevitable by-product of eating. He found defecating to be hideous. He vowed from then on never to use his own body, but rather to "possess" a "God-looking" man for his earthly visits. What if that man died? he briefly wondered. "Then I'll find another one who looks like him or I will devise a kind of 'man-suit' to wear, something like a deep-sea-diving suit, now no more questions!")

God, Abraham, and the two angels sat under a tree, eating quietly. The situation began to feel slightly awkward. God had never been in a social setting before; sitting there between the two angels and Abraham, the silence became terribly unpleasant to him. "I have to say something," he thought, and so he blurted out, "Sarah will soon give birth to a son named Isaac." Instantly, he felt foolish. He'd already told Abraham that; he was repeating himself. (Gen. 17:19, Gen. 18:10) Was that all he could come up with?

God heard laughter coming from the nearby tent. It was Sarah. She apparently found it funny that she would be having a baby at ninety years of age. God whipped around, glared at her. "Why is she laughing?" he demanded of Abraham. (He wasn't going to ask *her*, obviously.) "Is anything too wondrous for the Lord?" he said, feeling very good about talking of himself in third person, vowing to speak of himself that way more often in the future. (Gen. 18:13–14)

The woman—he'd already forgotten her name—was it Rachel?—quickly tried to lie to him: "I didn't laugh." But God knew she had. "Yes you did," he said. (Gen. 18:15) He considered killing her at that moment, having one of his angels beat her to death, but then he remembered that he'd just said she was going to give birth to Isaac, so he decided not to.

Also, quite honestly, God had bigger fish to fry. He and the angels were here to snuff out homosexuality, not have a strained picnic lunch (even if the veal was tremendous). When the angels moved on, Abraham walked with God, who decided to share the true purpose of his visit. Abraham asked God a brazen question: "Will you kill all the innocents too?" God stared at Abraham, taken aback. Abraham was questioning his wisdom? He thought of killing him too. Then he thought of telling him the truth: "*No one* is innocent, Abraham, you're *all* bad, it's just a matter of degree."

Finally, though, God decided to let it go. Someone had to become a great nation (Gen. 12:2), and it's not like God had a lot of great options. So he just nodded. "Fine, if there are fifty innocents, I will spare the town," he said. He knew there weren't *any* innocents in Sodom, that this whole conversation was moot. What if there were forty-five, Abraham pressed him . . . or forty . . . thirty . . . twenty . . . ten? (Gen. 18:28–32) Fine, fine, God said, knowing full well that he was going to destroy Sodom in any case and kill everyone there. But if it made Abraham feel better to think he was "saving" people, that was acceptable. Although, in truth, as the number kept dropping, God *did* start to feel a twinge of annoyance. "I'm going to play some sort of mean trick on Abraham in the near future," he thought.

God decided he'd had enough of being on earth. He flew back up to heaven (Gen. 18:23) and prepared to shoot fire down from the sky as soon as the moment was right. Which was going to be very soon, he could see, because down in Sodom everything was going exactly according to his plan. "Operation Eliminate Homosexuality is about to go down," God whispered to himself with a thin smile.

A mob of homosexuals appeared at Lot's door and started yelling, "Bring those men out so we can have sex with them!" (Gen. 19:5) God's jaw dropped—this was even worse than he'd expected! Not only were all the men in Sodom homosexuals, they were also rapists! They wanted to rape his angels ("exactly as I knew they would," he admitted to himself). God saw young boys in the mob, some as young as four or five—was that a two year-old?!—and found that puzzling. (Gen. 19:4) Were boys born homosexual in Sodom, he briefly wondered? "No," he instantly knew. "They *chose* it. It is an abomination and they will all die for it."

Lot tried to calm the mob by offering them his two virgin daughters for what would much later be crudely referred to as a "gangbang." (Gen. 19:8) But of course that wasn't going to work. "That mob of men wants penis and balls, not girls," God muttered to himself. He was slightly, uncomfortably excited by what was happening. There was a part of him, he had to admit, that actually wanted to see the mob rape his male angels. "Oh, they would, they *definitely* would," he whispered hoarsely, then shook his head slightly. "Focus, Lord," he told himself. "*Focus.*"

For a moment, God wondered whether what Lot had done, offering his virgin daughters to a rape-mob, was in any way "wrong." No, he decided, it was not. Lot *knew* all these men were homosexuals and wouldn't accept his offer, therefore it was not wrong. "It's not the homosexuals who want those girls," God chuckled to himself, "it's Lot himself!" And he would have them too!

God looked back down at Sodom. He'd taken his eye off it for a moment while he was thinking about Lot; the situation had deteriorated. The homosexual rapists were just about to break into Lot's house. (Gen. 19:9) "Time to move," God said to himself. He aimed a finger downward and instantly there was a blinding flash of light. (Gen. 19:11) The rapists staggered around, rubbing their eyes, suddenly helpless.

Lot grabbed his family and they rushed away. The angels told them not to look back (God wasn't totally sure why he didn't want them to look back; he just didn't, that's all), and when Lot's wife *did* look back, God took this opportunity to turn her into salt. (Gen. 19:26) It looked fantastic, better than he could have hoped—a bright white human statue, mouth agape, eyes wide. "A salty picture of terror," God thought to himself. (In years to come, animals would lick the salt sculpture down to nothing, which was both annoying and amusing to God.)

God sent holy fire down from the sky and burned up Sodom and Gomorrah and all the homosexuals who lived there. (Gen. 19:24) ("So much for our little 'deal,'" he smirked, thinking of Abraham.) It had been awhile since he had killed a bunch of humans at one time—since the flood really. As he watched all those sinners burn, shrieking and moaning in agony, God thought to himself, "This is good. This is what they deserve." He liked burning people—it was visual and exciting in a way that drowning them was not. Hell, he decided, when it was up and running, would be like this, except that rather than burning for 30 or 40 seconds, the wicked would burn *forever*. It was a delicious idea. Two little girls ran past, on fire. God stroked his mighty chin, wondering, did they have it coming too? Yes—yes, they did.

Lot and his daughters escaped to a cave where the old man had sex with both girls and impregnated them. Lot apparently felt slightly uncomfortable about what happened because he tried to lie and say it was the *girls'* idea, not his. (Gen. 19:32) "They got me drunk, I had no idea what was happening," he lied. "They told me that there were no other men on earth!" Which was ridiculous, God knew that very well; other than Sodom and Gomorrah, there were towns full of men everywhere! Lot had specifically asked for permission to take the girls to the next town! (Gen. 19:20) But God decided to let Lot get away with the story because, really . . . who cares? He had just wiped out the most abhorrent sin there was, homosexuality; what did he care if creepy old Lot wanted to have sex with his own daughters? As usual, God had no idea what their names were. (Gen. 19:31) "Women are so utterly boring to me!" he said to himself, amused. The sons that would result from these pregnancies, though, Moab and Ben-ami ("I always know the boys' names," God noted proudly to himself) would lead nations! That's how "wrong" Lot's behavior was! (Gen. 19:37–38)

When the two male angels returned to heaven, God looked at them and nodded, "well done." They really were distractingly handsome.

(A bit later, God got Abraham back for questioning his wisdom. "Kill your son, Isaac," he told him. God could barely keep a straight face at the old man's shocked reaction. God wasn't going to actually *allow* Isaac to be killed, obviously; the boy was quite important to him, in fact—but he was going to have fun with this practical joke, and he took it all the way. Abraham had the knife in the air, poised over his son, when God finally sent an angel down to stop him. "Abraham looked like he was going to shit his pants, it was hilarious!" God roared to some angels. "And I'll tell you something else too: He never talked back to me again!")

Chapter Nine

Time passed. Humans came and went. God, having, he felt, wiped out sin when he incinerated Sodom and Gomorrah, took a step back. "Let the humans figure things out for themselves for a while," he thought. Of course he knew they *wouldn't* figure things out, but he decided to let them try. (The truth was, he hadn't even wiped out towns full of homosexual rapists, it turned out!) (Jud. 19:22) Also, he had other things to work on. Hell, for instance, which was coming along nicely. It really was going to be spectacularly horrible. Heaven too. God's home in the sky had started out as basically nothingness floating over water. Boooo-ring.

Now God had begun to work on it and as he did, he realized that he had very specific tastes, and that he loved it. It was gaudy and colorful and *fabulous*. Heaven was becoming the wonderful home he'd always wanted for himself. Designing and decorating it took a *lot* of time and effort, though. At the center of things, there was a massive marble sculpture of God, one hand raised, the other on his hip, a stern look on his face. It was marvelous. There were also lots and lots of mirrors; God loved mirrors. There were, as well, a number of heroic portrait paintings of God hanging in midair. Most of them had been painted by angels, who were not particularly gifted artists (most of them, God much later realized, were mildly retarded), but no matter, they were still excellent.

One of the few times God looked down at what was happening on earth, he saw a man named Onan, who refused to impregnate his sister-in-law, pulling out before he ejaculated. (Gen. 38:9) This was absolutely unacceptable! Sperm was precious stuff, *not* to be spilled on the ground! Onan would also sometimes masturbate, which God was infuriated by. "That glorious seed is not to be wasted!" he nearly shouted as he watched Onan "whack off." God killed Onan, obviously. (Gen. 38:10)

After several hundred years of working on heaven, as well as traveling around the universe he'd created ("not much," he thought to himself), God felt reenergized, ready to reengage with mankind. It was around this time that a human being came along who God liked in a wholly different way than any he'd known before. The man's name was Moses, and he was smart, tough, ambitious, and loyal. For the first time, God thought to himself, "This is a guy I'd like to be friends with." Moses, naturally, felt the same way, and so a beautiful friendship was born. "This guy understands me," God would think to himself. "I can express myself with him! I can tell him exactly how I want my people to act!"

Their friendship had gotten off to a very rocky start. Moses had not cut off his own son's foreskin, as God had demanded, and God was furious about it. "I like Moses very much, but that foreskin of his son's *has* to go," he had thought. God *hated* foreskins. "My biggest mistake," he had called them. "I should send Moses a message," God had thought. "Get your son circumcised *immediately*." Yes, that was the obvious thing for him to do. But then God shook his head violently. "No. I'm going to *kill Moses*," he had suddenly decided. (Ex. 4:24) "I like him and I want to be friends with him, but this foreskin thing is too much. I'm going to beat him to death with my bare hands."

God flew down to earth and walked toward his peoples' camp. It was night, very dark. There were a few small fires burning, a few quiet voices. God stomped toward the camp, clenching his fists. Suddenly he stopped, feeling his foot sink into something soft and squishy. The smell hit him. He looked down. It was human poo! God cursed; he had to remember to command the humans to bury their poo! (Deut. 23:14–15) It was all over his sandal! God was even *more* furious now. He *hated* the humans at this moment, the way they pooped on the ground, the way they disobeyed him, the way they didn't remove their foreskins!

God saw someone walking toward him from the camp. It was Moses! God charged him and tackled him, knocking him to the ground with a heavy thud. Moses looked up, amazed. "God?" he managed, before God punched him in the face, *hard*. Moses' head spun to one side, his eyes rolled, a trickle of blood ran out of his nose. God hit him again in the mouth, crack! Moses' lip split; blood ran between his teeth. "What are you *doing?*" Moses whispered, before God grabbed him by the throat and started to squeeze. "I'm going to kill you, Moses," he said between clenched teeth. He slowly throttled Moses, feeling the life ebb out of him. God hesitated. Was he really going to kill Moses, the future lawgiver, just because his son still had a foreskin? Yes, he was, *definitely*. Moses' eyes bugged out, his face was purple, he was nearly dead.

Then God heard frantic footsteps rushing toward him and a woman's voice screaming "wait, WAIT!" As God pulled back for a second and Moses sucked in a desperate breath, his wife, Zipporah, her son in her arms, rushed between her husband and God. Wielding a sharp rock, she very quickly and efficiently proceeded to yank up her son's little robe and cut off his foreskin! (Ex. 4:25) God sat back, out of breath, amazed at Zipporah's actions. Somehow, from inside their tent, she had grasped that God was throttling her husband to death because their son still had a foreskin. Grabbing a rock ("a *rock*," God marveled), she had rushed out and, in near darkness, cut the wailing baby's foreskin off! She had then rubbed the bloody foreskin against Moses' leg and said to him, "Now you are truly a bridegroom of blood." God got up and, without a word, walked back into the desert night, trying to understand Zipporah's odd remark but failing.

Then he flew up to heaven and cleaned the last bit of shit out of his sandal.

God was glad Moses was still alive. In Moses, he finally had someone he could open up to—someone he could share his desires for his people with and also trust to communicate that vision to others. "I could just appear in the sky, I suppose," God mused to himself. "Talk to all of them at once." It wasn't a bad idea exactly—but he didn't want to do it. He wanted to talk to *one person*, Moses, and then have *him* talk to all the other people. It just felt better that way, and by this point God had learned to not second guess himself.

Moses traveled back to Egypt, and this gave God the chance to mess with Pharaoh again. He had enjoyed causing plagues back in Abraham's day, "but that was nothing," God grinned to himself. "This time, Pharaoh is *really* going to pay." ("For what?" popped into his head. "*For not believing in me*," came the instant response, followed a second later by, "Exactly according to my plan!")

God pondered how he would torment Pharaoh. "If he will not allow my people to worship me—which he won't, I will *see* to it that he doesn't!—(God could control Pharaoh's mind and make him do whatever he wanted, "like a puppet," he chuckled to himself) (Ex. 7:3)—then I will plague him with . . . hmm, what?" God stroked his chin, thinking of the *worst* things he could send at Pharaoh. Snakes? Wasps? Spiders? Suddenly he snapped his fingers; "I have it!" he exclaimed. "I will send a plague of frogs at Pharaoh!" (Ex. 7:27) God despised frogs—their slimy skin, popped out eyes, and hideous croaking. God would send them into Pharaoh's palace. That would teach him!

The plague of frogs worked brilliantly, Pharaoh begged to have the frogs removed. (Ex. 8:4) God told Moses to warn Pharaoh that the plagues were just beginning. "I could kill you if I wanted to," God had Moses tell Pharaoh. "The only reason I don't is because I want you to see my power, so I will become more famous!" (Ex. 9:16) God was slightly surprised by what he'd just said. He wanted to be famous? He was the creator of the entire universe, why would "fame" matter to him? Immediately God moved on. "So I want fame, so what?"

Pharaoh softened a little; he was about to let God's people do what they wanted. But that was no good. God wanted to keep punishing Pharaoh; he loved punishing him; he had no interest in ending what he by now called "my little hurting game." So every single time Pharaoh came close to doing exactly what God demanded of him, God hardened his heart and forced him *not* to do it! (Ex. 10:1, 10:20, 10:27, 11:10, 14:4, 14:8) For a moment, God considered the idea of "free will." That is, did humans have it? If God could mind-control Pharaoh, the most powerful man in the world, who *couldn't* he control? Answer: No one—he controlled everyone. But if the humans weren't free, if he was controlling them, then on what basis was he punishing them? "Am I not the puppeteer who hates his own puppets?" God asked himself, then quickly answered: "Indeed I do hate them and I'll tell you why: Because they are wicked!" Problem solved.

"Now I will kill all the firstborn Egyptian children," God thought to himself, tickled by the idea. (Ex. 11:4–5) Pharaoh obviously wanted to relent by this time, but God wouldn't let him. God had his angels sneak into all the Egyptian houses and smother the children. (Ex. 12:29) He also had a few firstborn cows killed. (Unfortunately, the meat went bad by the time the angels got it back to heaven.)

God's "Operation Mass-Child-Murder" was a huge success. Pharaoh decided to let God's people go, which was exactly what Moses had been asking for. "I'll accept the victory," God thought at first—then changed his mind. "For one thing, I am not *quite* famous enough yet," he thought. "For another thing, I freaking love punishing Pharaoh and I am *still* not ready to be done." God made his Pharaoh-puppet pursue the Hebrews toward the Red Sea. Looking down, he rubbed his hands together in anticipation. "Double back," God told Moses. "Trick Pharaoh into *thinking* you're lost, so that he will attack you." (Ex. 14:1–4)

Which is exactly what happened. God parted the sea, allowing his people to cross. Then, when the Egyptians pursued them, he "unparted" it, drowning them all! (Ex. 14:27–28) It was fantastic, like the old days. "I'd forgotten how much I enjoy drowning people," God nodded to himself.

God considered telling Moses to return to Egypt yet again, so that he could torment Pharaoh some more; he had an idea that pertained to swollen anuses that he was anxious to try out. But he decided he had more important work to do with his people.

It was time to lay down the law.

Chapter Ten

God started with the most important thing: Number one—Do *not* worship any god other than me. ("I could stop there, honestly," he thought to himself, but decided to go on.) Number two—Really don't worship any other gods. Number three—Don't use my name in vain. (Ex. 20:3–7)

After that, God thought for a minute. What else did he have? Oh, here was one: Number four—Take one day a week off, just like I did when I made the universe. What else? Several came in a rush now: Number five—Respect your parents; Number six—Don't kill people; Number seven—No sex outside marriage; Number eight—Don't steal; Number nine—Don't lie, and . . . . What was the last one? Don't rape women? No, not that. Don't keep people as slaves? No. Don't abuse children or animals? *No no no.* Later, God would remember that what he had meant to say was: Number ten—Don't eat mice (Lev. 11:29)—but it had slipped his mind, so he said "Don't be jealous of each other" instead. Which was fine too. (Ex. 20:4–14)

And that was it, he was done. God sat back and crossed his arms, quite confident that these ten rules ("commandments," he quickly corrected himself) would be all the guidance his people would need. Then, annoyingly, who should show up to talk about how hell was coming along but Satan. And, as always, he asked ridiculous questions. "Don't you think they already *knew* you didn't want them to worship any other gods?" he asked.

"So what if they did, Satan? I was *clarifying*," God said, exasperated. "Besides, it wasn't all about me. I gave them some excellent laws! Respect your parents, for instance."

"Don't they do that already?"

"What?"

"Don't they already respect their parents? Don't human beings naturally do that?"

"What are you driving at, Satan?"

"Aren't you just 'commanding' them to do things they already do?"

God was incensed by this line of questioning. He had felt so confident before Satan arrived, but now . . . his body tightened as Satan continued, smiling pleasantly.

"The same with 'don't kill' and 'don't steal.' Don't they already know those things are wrong?"

"Not until my commandments they didn't!"

"Also, you tell them not to kill *now*, but aren't you going to *want* them to kill quite soon?" (Num. 31:37)

God glared at Satan, deeply irritated by his presumptions. His Ten Commandments were excellent, he knew that, and now Satan was mocking them. "I really should destroy him right here, right now," God thought to himself. He was thinking of how he'd do it—throttle him?—impale him?—but then he had second thoughts. He took a breath, nodded, smiled coolly. "How is hell coming along?" he asked.

"A bit slower than expected," Satan said. "It won't be ready for another hundred earth years."

"But it's going to be horrible?"

"Extremely horrible."

"I want it to be excruciating for them—*agonizing*."

"It will be."

"Good, good."

There was a strained pause. God and Satan looked at each other; God shifted his weight a little. Why did he always have the awful feeling that Satan was laughing at him? Like he saw something and was amused by it. Which was infuriating. He was *God*, he demanded respect and obedience, he had created Satan and he was not going to be mocked by him. God nodded brusquely. "You may go now."

Satan looked at God, nodded, and turned away without saying another word. As God watched him go, he seethed. "His criticism of my Ten Commandments was ridiculous." But he *did* start thinking of other laws for the humans. "Only to supplement what I already told them," he told himself.

"When a man sells his daughter as a slave," God told Moses soon thereafter, "she should not be freed as male slaves are." (Ex. 21:7) It was a good law, God thought. But there was a part of him that briefly wondered: "Shouldn't I tell Moses that it's *wrong* for a father to sell his daughter as a slave in the first place?" He thought this over for a moment. *Was* it wrong for a father to sell his daughter as a slave? God was "laying down the law" here and he wanted to get it right (which he knew he would, in any case, because he was perfect), so he asked himself again, "Is there anything wrong with a father selling his daughter as a slave?" The answer came quickly: There was nothing wrong with it, nothing in the least! "We're talking about *girls* here," God chuckled to himself.

More ideas started coming to God. "If a child insults his mother or father, he should be put to death," he told Moses. (Ex. 21:17) Another good law—strong and fierce and hard. He'd already stated that children should respect their parents, but he hadn't made clear what the punishment would be if they didn't. Now he had: *Death.* Again, God had brief second thoughts. Was there something . . . hmm . . . *unreasonable* about this law? No, not at all. *Authority* mattered and parents were earthly authorities—or fathers were anyway (maybe it was okay to insult mothers?), and anyone who criticized authority should be killed. This seemed obvious to God. "How should they be killed?" God asked himself, stroking his chin—then nodded, knowing the answer: Throw rocks at their heads. (Deut. 21:21)

God was on a roll now. "When an ox gores a person to death, the ox should be stoned," he told Moses. (Ex. 21:28) Again—*obvious*. The ox had done something wicked and needed to be punished for it. But again, God hesitated for a second. Was an ox capable of the kind of moral transgression that required "punishment?" Why not just slaughter it? Why stone it to death? "Because," God announced, "some oxen choose to gore people to death!" Along the same lines, all those animals that were choosing to have sex with humans, or even thinking about it? They needed to be stoned too! Damned slutty goats, damned lascivious donkeys! They all had bloodguilt upon them! (Lev. 20:16)

Now God began to feel a different impulse. "Enough about *them*," he found himself thinking. "I want to talk about *me*, I want to tell Moses what *I* want!"

God had been working on heaven for awhile and it was coming along fantastically well; a work-in-progress, sure, but you could see how utterly amazing it was going to be. Now God turned his sights to earth. It had been so drab up to this point; God wanted it to be brighter, more colorful and spectacular. "I know exactly how I want my temple to look." God told Moses to demand that people bring him gifts: Gold, silver, copper, linen, fur, oils, spices, incense, pretty rocks—the works. (Ex. 25:2)

God had created the Grand Canyon and Mount Everest, not to mention Saturn (none of which he seemed to know existed, but never mind that), so in a way he felt a bit weird asking for incense and rocks. But that feeling didn't last long. He liked these things. They were the finest things earth had to offer and he would use them to have the humans create a shrine to him that would be absolutely breathtaking. God knew that Satan would describe his taste as ostentatious and showy. He didn't care at all. "Let him think I have the taste of a fruity old queen," he said. "What do I care?" And it was true, he didn't, not in the least. He liked gold balls and pomegranate blue fabric and cherubs and lots of incense—and so what? (Ex. 25:18, 28:33–34)

It felt so good, so *liberating*. God had worked hard creating the universe, then spent a lot of time and energy coming up with perfect laws for his humans to live by. Which was all rewarding, sure—but what about *him*, what about *his* needs? God felt that he was, in some deeply symbolic sense, "coming out of a closet," and it felt wonderful. All along, God now realized, he had wanted two things: Fabulousness and spectacle! Now, finally, he was getting them.

God was feeling more and more comfortable with expressing himself now. ("I was so repressed," he fretted briefly before shrugging it off. "But not anymore!") "I'm even going to tell Moses exactly how I want meat grilled! I will tell him what kind of flour to use and what kind of oil—I will even tell him what kind of wine to serve it with!" (Ex. 29:40, Num. 15:7)

God was happy. His people were finally giving him what he wanted: A fancy shrine and well-cooked meat. All was well. Or as well as it could be, given that humans—even *his* humans— were essentially evil and corrupt creatures. He probably should have drowned them all in the flood—but oh well, he didn't, and now he'd promised not to.

Chapter Eleven

Moses was a good friend. Ever since their rocky start, when God had tried to kill him, things had gone really well between them. God felt comfortable with Moses, at ease. For the first time, he felt understood. Moses' brother Aaron, though? Well, he was a different story. Aaron was tough enough—a good disciplinarian and fighter. But he was kind of an idiot too.

What had been God's first commandment, his very *first*? "Do *not* worship other gods." So what did Aaron do while God and Moses were up in the hills, talking? He melted down a bunch of gold ("which really should have been used for my temple," God fumed) and created a golden cow to worship! (Ex. 32:2–4) "I should kill Aaron," God thought. "No, wait—I should kill *all* of them." And he was about to do it too, he really was (Ex. 32:10), when Moses talked him down a little bit, as only good and trusted friends can do.

"If you kill everybody," Moses asked, "what will the Egyptians think of you?" (Ex. 32:12) This was an excellent question. What would they think (specifically, what would *Pharaoh* think) if God killed all his own people? It's true, he could puppet the Egyptians into admiring him, but he didn't want to do that. He wanted them to admire him for being himself, even if they were wicked and evil and destined for eternal punishment. He hadn't worked so hard for fame to simply throw it away in such a cavalier way.

So God decided not to kill the entire tribe. Moses did kill several thousand people for God, which was a good consolation prize. (Ex. 32:28) God sent a plague after that, which was satisfying too. (Ex. 32:35) "But I didn't kill them all," God noted to himself, feeling generous.

A bit later, God and Moses were talking again. God had taken the shape of a cloud—he liked to do things like that—he was a bush another time (Ex. 3:4)—and he found himself saying to Moses, "The Lord, the Lord—a God compassionate and gracious, slow to anger, abounding in faithfulness and kindness." (Ex. 34:6) Moses was silent. God felt odd for a moment. Had that sounded weird, the way he'd complimented himself in third person? He wasn't sure. He didn't think so. Everything he had said was true, obviously, but did it sound . . . insecure? What kind of God praises his own kindness and compassion in third person, he couldn't help wondering. Then, quickly, he knew the answer to that question: The kind of God who doesn't get *enough* praise and admiration from his own people, THAT'S WHO! "If they won't talk about how compassionate I am, then *I* will, and if that's insecure, then so be it!"

Still, the little voice in his mind whispered: "But why do I feel the need to remind people that I'm God so often? Who said I *wasn't*?" A disturbing thought: Was he so insecure that he doubted himself? That he somehow feared the humans were onto him and tried to maintain his position through bluster and intimidation? No. No no no.

Moving on, God felt that he needed to clarify something important with Moses. "All fat is the Lord's," he told him. (Lev. 3:16) The humans had been cutting God out of his share of fat; they had been consuming it themselves and that was unacceptable, fat was *his*, ALL of it. ("What do you do with all that fat, God?" Satan asked him once. "Do you make candles?" God wouldn't even dignify this with the true answer—which was that he liked to eat fat.)

Next on the agenda, God needed to tell his people what

was good for them to eat and what wasn't. God had by this time sampled almost every kind of grilled meat there was; he considered himself something of a connoisseur. He began with what was *good*: Anything that lived in water was fine, unless it didn't have fins or scales—in other words, if it wasn't a fish. In which case it was bad—no, that wasn't a sufficient word— he knew the right word—anything else was an abomination. (Lev. 11:12) Lobsters, for example? Abominations. Crabs? Abominations. Anything that lived in a shell? *Abominations!* "Why did I make them?" God briefly wondered. "Did I make them? I don't seem to have made reptiles—is it possible that Satan made reptiles *and* lobsters?" God decided that it was not possible: He had made everything, and if some of the things he'd made were abominations to him—well, what of it? He liked what he liked and hated what he hated. (Still, the question—could Satan have created lobsters?—did stick in his mind for a while.)

God moved on to birds. "You may eat any bird you want!" he told Moses, then quickly added, "other than eagles, vultures, hawks, ravens, and bats." (Lev. 11:19) There was an awkward pause. Had he just called bats birds? He had, yes. That was embarrassing. Obviously God knew that bats were mammals. What kind of God wouldn't know *that*? He'd simply been talking too fast and out it came: "Bats are birds." Moses didn't say anything, he just stood there, looking down. "What should I say?" God wondered. "Should I say, 'That thing I just said about bats being birds? Obviously that's not correct, bats are mammals, of course. The *point* I was trying to make was, you know, don't eat them. They're abominations.'" No, it sounded weak, not like something an all-knowing and all-powerful creator would say. Could he say, "I was kidding when I said that bats were birds," or "I was just testing you, Moses?"

God decided not to say anything, to simply move on. So what if he'd called bats birds? It was meaningless. He moved on to insects, most of which he regarded as abominations. He'd made a lot of them (especially beetles for some unknown reason), but he mainly thought they were repulsive. None of them were good to eat, God proclaimed—before remembering a few exceptions. "You may eat locusts, crickets, and grasshoppers," he announced to Moses. (Lev. 11:22) God had tried eating each of these bugs and found them to be surprisingly tasty and nutritious and crunchy.

God imagined his mental checklist: Lobsters and shrimp? Abominations. Bat-birds? Same. ("Wrong! Bats aren't birds, I know that!") Crickets? Good eating. Was that it? No, he had some other regulations: "Don't eat mice," he finally got around to telling Moses. He had not actually seen any of his people eating mice, but he wasn't taking any chances. Mice were . . . unclean. God liked things that were clean—like grasshoppers. The idea of his people eating filthy little mice sickened him. "Don't eat moles either," God told Moses (Lev. 11:29)—revolting little eyeless freaks. And lizards—do not eat lizards—they are abominations.

God really hated unclean things like mice and, honestly? . . . menstruating women. (Lev. 12:2) That was not what he and Moses were talking about, he knew that, but still—menstruating women were so damned unclean. God hadn't trusted women from the start, but this whole monthly bleeding thing—it was awful. (Not long after this, God made clear what he'd always felt was obvious: "Women are worth 60% of what men are worth," he told Moses, thinking to himself as he said it, "which is being *generous*.") (Lev. 27:3–4) God didn't want to get stuck on the whole "menstruating women are unclean" thing—even though it was true—so he moved on to medical matters for a moment.

Existing outside time and space, as God obviously did, he had a perfect understanding of human illness. With regard to leprosy, God advised Moses that the best treatment was to kill a bird and sprinkle its blood on the leper. (Lev. 14:5–7) As Moses wrote this down, God nodded to himself and murmured, "Right on the money, Lord."

God tried to get back to food—but his mind started to feel contaminated now. So *many* of the things he'd created were unclean: shrimp, mice, bat-birds ("stop!"), menstruating women, lepers. Yes, he'd made some things that were clean, like locusts and catfish and goats—but still—even the things that were clean so often had blemishes. God hated blemishes. He wanted perfection. "I am perfect and I created this world, so *it* should be perfect too!" he reasoned with impeccable logic. "Why should I have to tolerate so many blemishes?" he demanded. And not just any kind of blemish either; many of the flaws were in the worst place they could possibly be: The balls. (Lev. 22:24)

God loved perfect balls. Perfect, hanging, unblemished balls. But they were so very rare. ("Especially in combination with a perfect, cut penis," he murmured to himself.) There were goats that were perfect except for their balls, which were bruised, torn, cut, whatever. These goats were of *zero* interest to God. "I only want the ones with perfect balls!" he would demand. "I also only want to be served by men with perfect balls!" (Lev. 21:20)

By the time he was done laying down the law, God felt confident. He had made it clear what he expected of his people, what was clean, what was unclean, the importance of perfect balls, all of it.

"Things should fall into place nicely now," he thought.

Chapter Twelve

But it was strange.

Problems continued—bad ones: (1) Sin was back. God had tried so hard to wipe it out, drowning everyone on earth, incinerating two cities. But for some reason it was rampant once again. His people were having sex with animals now, for instance. (Lev. 18:23) And perhaps one of the reasons for *that* was (2) God's people, his chosen ones, were starting to drift toward other gods. (Lev. 20:2) God hated all these made-up gods, but the one who he truly despised was Baal, the so-called sex god. People loved Baal; he was seductive, even to God's own people. (Num. 25:1–3) Baal didn't exist, obviously, "But if he *did*, I would definitely kill him," God muttered to himself. (Much later, when God discovered that Baal actually *did* exist, he would kill him, along with all the other, *not*-made-up-as-it-turned-out gods. The moment when God shoved his knife into Baal's gut and felt his life flow out was very rewarding.) (Isa. 26:13–14)

"Why am I so bothered by a fictional character?" God would sometimes wonder. "I'm God, why should I be threatened by someone that doesn't even exist? I shouldn't be . . . and you know what, I'm not." God would then sit in tense silence for awhile, fretting about this. There were moments when he couldn't help but wonder: "Why did I create a reality that makes me so damned angry?" He was mad all the time, it seemed. His people infuriated him—they didn't listen, they didn't obey, they did wicked, evil things and worst of all, they worshipped that asshole, Baal.

On top of all that, bizarre things were happening. Ghosts, for instance. God didn't like ghosts—he didn't like anything about them. He had created them, obviously—but now he'd forgotten why. "It must have seemed like a good idea at the time," he reflected, "to have dead people continue to wander the earth as semitransparent, floating entities." It must have been designed as some kind of punishment, God decided (what *wasn't?*), but it hadn't worked out the way he'd wanted. He didn't want humans and ghosts to interact with each other. "Anyone who has a ghost," God informed Moses, "shall be put to death." (Lev. 20:27) "Won't that just create *more* ghosts?" flashed across his mind, but he dismissed it instantly, muttering "ludicrous" to himself as he did.

His creatures were scared of death. God knew that. Even if ghosts didn't exist, humans would probably have made them up to comfort themselves. Humans did things like that—devising stories and characters to make themselves feel better and less afraid. It was touching in a way and for a moment, God softened. "It's not easy being human," he said to himself. "It's quite frightening apparently. Death scares them terribly and they need to find ways to comfort themselves." Still, was he supposed to just let it pass? No. Anyone who talked to a ghost needed to have large rocks hurled at their head until they were dead. It was the only thing to do.

These problems were frustrating to God because what he wanted to be doing was giving his people advice on important matters like—well, sideburns, for instance! "You shall not destroy the side growth of your beard," he told Moses. (Lev. 19:27) God liked sideburns—*loved* them, actually. Most of his angels had them and he thought they looked quite virile. "Destroying them is a sin," God thought. That's how he put it—not "cutting them off," but "destroying them." (God sometimes wondered if he would look good with sideburns. He decided he would, very much so.)

"I also want to give them advice on buying and selling houses!" God proclaimed—and so he did. (Lev. 25:29–30) This felt, he had to admit, slightly trivial, given that he was God and all. ("Is it like Abraham Lincoln adding skin-care advice to the Gettysburg Address?" he wondered. No, that was completely wrong. For one thing, Lincoln wouldn't even exist for another 3,000 years! For another, what if he *did* offer skin-care advice in the Gettysburg Address? Would that be so bad?)

Again and again, maddeningly, God had to command his mulish, recalcitrant people to obey him. "If you do obey me," he told them, "you will be untroubled by enemies, including wild animals." (Lev. 26:6) ("Can I really promise that?" he briefly wondered.) "But if you *don't* obey me . . ." God considered what he wanted to say to his people, then nodded, having found the perfect thing: "If you *don't* obey me, I will send wild animals to eat your children." *That* should do it, he thought. But just to be *s*ure, he added "I will also make you eat your own children." (Lev. 26:22–29)

God smiled, thinking of how his people would react to that one. "We don't want to eat our own children!" they would wail. Which was his point, obviously. Obey me and you won't have to! Disobey me and you will! There was little doubt this would work; humans had zero desire to eat their own children, God knew that. But *just in case* they still wanted to disobey, God lowered the boom on them.

"If you don't obey me," he told Moses, pausing for effect . . . "I will no longer savor your pleasing odors." (Lev. 26:31) God chuckled, thinking about how that one would land.

"Why isn't God asking us to grill meat for him anymore?"

"He no longer savors the smell!!"

"Noooooooooooooo!!"

Chapter Thirteen

God thought he'd straightened everything out with his "eat your own children" threat—but there seemed to be something almost beyond reach in many of his people. They were proud, stubborn, *difficult*. No matter what God said or did, they seemed . . . unconvinced. That made him seethe. "I chose one small group of people on the entire planet to be mine and even most of them doubt my words!"

God felt especially bad for Moses. People had the temerity to question whether he was the only one who could talk to God! (Num. 12:2) "Anyone can claim to be talking to God," they would say. "We can all talk to God, not just you, Moses." Which was utterly absurd! God had chosen Moses to talk to; when other people talked to him, he ignored them. He had no interest in talking to anyone else! "I'm going to kill them all," God decided.

Once again, Moses talked him down: "What will people think of you? What will the *Egyptians* think of you?" he asked—which was, you know, always an effective question. ("Why do I care so damned much what Pharaoh thinks of me?" crossed God's mind for a moment.) Fine, God wouldn't kill everybody, but *something* had to be done. Rebellion against Moses simply could not be allowed! Even Moses was starting to feel the pressure. "Why have you laid all this on me?" he asked God

(Num. 11:11), who briefly considered flying down and beating him to death for that. "I need to straighten things out," God thought to himself, then nodded decisively. "I will appear before all the tribal elders and speak to them."

"How should I appear before them?" God asked himself. "Given that some are doubting me, shouldn't I show up as a man, as I have several times before (Ex. 33:11), and prove myself to them?" He stroked his chin, then shook his head firmly. Too obvious. He would appear to the elders as a cloud. That was better, much more convincing. Should he then *talk* to the elders as the cloud? No, he had a far better idea than that. He would, as the cloud, excite the elders so much that they would speak in a kind of excited gibberish! (Num. 11:25)

If God's people were reasonable at all (which they were *not*, needless to say) this would have convinced them of the truth of what Moses was saying. But of course, as God knew beforehand, it would not convince them. Before long, they would be complaining again: "We want to go back to Egypt, we don't like it here, *waaaah*." (Num. 14:2–4) God decided to punish them preemptively for this whining. "I will give them a huge windfall of meat," he thought. "But guess what? The meat will be poisoned, haha!" So God blew a bunch of quail into camp. His people feasted on them and a lot of them died. (Num. 11:31–33)

"I cloud-inspired old men to speak gibberish and *still* they doubted me, so I had no choice but to kill a bunch of them, including some who were not even opposed to Moses and so what?" God told his angels, feeling completely justified in his behavior. The angels agreed with him absolutely.

God decided to punish his people further by sending them into battle against the Amalekites. Now make no mistake: God *hated* the Amalekites, despised them really. (Ex. 17:14–16) He wanted them wiped out; even the memory of them he wanted wiped out, and he had vowed to *do it* too! But before he did that, he would use them to punish his own people. (Num. 15:43–

45) "My subtlety sometimes amazes even me," God thought to himself.

But *that* didn't work either. The discontent about Moses' authority continued, even increased. There were four ringleaders now—Korah, Dathan, Abiram, and Om—spearheading a group of several hundred people. God was furious. He really *was* going to kill all of them. And this time, there was nothing that Moses could say to stop him. The only question was how to kill them. Should he burn them up? Drown them? Have them eaten by wild animals? Force them to eat *each other*?

No. God had a better idea, a spectacular idea, a "home run," he would later call it. "I will cause the earth to open up beneath their feet and *swallow them*," he cried happily. And not just the four ringleaders either—God was going to kill their entire families too, little children and all. (Num. 16:30–33) "I am sick and tired of this endless carping, I intend to put an end to it, once and for all," he told his angels, who agreed that this was exactly the right thing to do. "After the earth swallows up those opposed to my boy Moses and deposits them in sheol—well, *that* should do it!" he announced. God wished that "hell" was ready for these troublemakers; eternal fire was what they deserved, and it was slightly frustrating that all they'd get was sort of grey endless nothingness. But no matter. The looks on their faces as they felt the ground beneath them open up would be priceless.

Needless to say, *this* plan would not "work" either, God knew that—but that was fine. As for the rest of the rebels, God shot fire down from the sky and finished them off. (Num. 16:35) The rebellion was squashed. Things were back on track.

Except that they weren't.

Even after God's astonishing "Five point plan" to quell the rebellion: (1) Appear as a cloud and cause old men to speak gibberish; (2) Blow bad birdmeat into camp to poison people; (3) Use the Amalekites to kick his people's asses; (4) Open the earth to swallow rebel leaders and their families; (5) Fireblast two hundred others—the griping *continued*. The people *still* complained about Moses' leadership, still doubted him, still wanted to return to Egypt. (Num. 17:6) God was stunned. "What is it going to take to get their attention?" he marveled. He decided to send another plague, which killed 15,000 more people. (Num. 17:14)

There were moments when God almost couldn't *believe* what he was seeing. Even after the plague, after 15,000 deaths, people still—*STILL*—complained. (Num. 21:5) What was wrong with them? There were moments when the old dark questions crossed his mind again: "Did I really create all this? If so, why do I seem to have so little power to influence things? What's wrong with me? Am I inept? Am I a fraud? Am I crazy?"

God took a deep breath, calmed himself. None of those things were true. He was all-knowing, all-powerful, and all-good. The problem, as he had already noted on several occasions, was with humans. They were bad, disobedient, and proud. They deserved *more* punishment, and he would give it to them. (Fuck it, he loved giving it to them.) "If the plague that killed 15,000 of them didn't stop the complaining, then I will send poisonous snakes—possibly fire snakes—to bite them!" he thundered. (Num. 21:8)

This time, however, as God watched his people moaning in agony about their snake bites, he took pity on them. "I have punished them enough for a while," he told his angels. "I will be merciful now." He instructed Moses to build a big copper snake which would cure the bites. (Num. 21:9) Was he being inconsistent, God wondered. After all, he had condemned "false idols" over and over again, it was basically his second commandment (Ex. 20:4), and now he was having his people more or less worship a big copper serpent. Was that odd at all? "I work in mysterious ways," God told himself, enjoying, as usual, the way that sounded.

God's people did behave better for a while. They took the town of Bashan, ruled by King Og (the name made God laugh every time he heard it. "I am King Og!" he would snort to

THE STORY OF GOD • 71

himself), and per God's instructions, killed everyone in it. God
was amazed how little the deaths of nonbelievers mattered to
him. Old women impaled? Babies dashed on rocks? Ho hum.
(Num. 31:15–17; Isa. 9:17; Isa. 13:18) For a moment, God began
to think that maybe—*maybe*—his people had *finally* learned their
lesson.

How wrong he was.

Not long after taking Bashan, the men—his men—*God's
men*—started having sex with, to be blunt, *whores*. (Non-Israelite
women, that is. God called any woman who wasn't an Israelite a
whore, which she was. Many Israelite women were whores too,
to be honest. Most women were whores, when you got down
to it.) And that wasn't even the worst of it; the men also started
flirting with the whore's god, who happened to be . . . Baal!
(Num. 25:1–3) "What is the point of all this?" God began to
wonder. "Why do I waste my time with these people? They're
hopeless." This was never going to work, ever. He should pull
the plug on the whole thing and move on. Maybe start over
on another planet somewhere. There were plenty that would
support life, God knew that. Why not do it? "I should, you
know—I really should. I should just kill them all, send them to
hell—which is nearing completion—and move on. That's the
sensible thing to do."

But he just couldn't get himself to do it. As much as God
hated humans—and he did, they were awful—he couldn't help
but feel . . . what was it? Not love exactly, he definitely didn't *love*
them . . . but attachment. He felt *attached* to them. He'd created
this whole thing for them. They'd been through a lot together.
He wasn't ready to throw in the towel on the whole thing. "I
can still make this work," he told himself. "I have lots of ideas I
haven't even tried yet—big ideas, great ideas!"

Also, he didn't claim to have "perfect self-understanding";
he was God, he was complicated, multifaceted. If, for whatever
reason, he needed his plan to fail utterly for a very long time—
well, he must have good reason for wanting that! "The satisfaction

will be all the greater once I decide I *want* things to go as I say I want them to!" he told himself.

God had all the men who were involved in worshipping Baal impaled: Problem solved. (Num. 25:4) Things got back on track again for a while. His people attacked the Midianites and defeated them. At first, they wanted to spare the women and children, but God straightened them out. "Kill everyone except the girls, then divide the booty," he told Moses. (Num. 31:27)

"Was that a crude way of putting it?" he asked one of his angels. "Did I sound like a pirate or something when I said 'booty'? Would it be like the Buddha (who was a fake, needless to say, but just as an example) saying, 'Kick the shit out of that guy?'" The angel assured God that he'd expressed himself perfectly—as God already knew he had, in truth.

Chapter Fourteen

God's people were on the verge of success now. He had led them to the River Jordan and they were poised to take the land that was rightfully theirs from the people that lived there. God thought it was funny that other people thought this land was "theirs." That was ridiculous, of course; the land belonged to his people and they were just about to take it. The only problem was . . . his people didn't seem to want to fight. (Deut. 1:26) God commanded them to go take their land, but they refused.

God stood there with his hands on his hips for a moment, staring down, speechless. These people were unbelievable. God had intended to help them defeat their enemies, but now he changed his mind. By the time Moses finally shamed them into fighting, God had decided he didn't want to help them anymore. Yes, he wanted them to take their land—he'd led them a long way to do so. But their laziness and cowardice infuriated him. He would let them lose. (Deut. 1:42–44) "Maybe that will teach them," he told himself (knowing as he said it that it would not, that nothing would teach them; that they would never ever learn.)

God's people fought and, exactly as he wished, lost. Moses then spent a long time trying to inspire them to fight again. "Good luck," God thought, annoyed. "My people drive me crazy," he told some angels. "I brought them to the brink of success and they *still* don't listen to me, it's galling." God wondered if he should take a look at other parts of the world to see if there were other people who might appeal to him. No, he decided—these few thousand men in this one small part of the world were the only ones that interested him. He decided to continue working with them. Also, he liked Moses very much. He truly wanted to see him take Canaan before he died. "In the end, I will *not* allow him that," God declared. "But I do want to." (Deut. 1:37)

As long as he was sticking around, not going to visit another solar system or something, God decided to teach his people a few more important lessons: "Don't eat rabbits," he commanded Moses. (Deut. 14:7) "Vile little hopping abominations," he muttered to himself. "Among birds, don't eat bats," God reiterated—then silently kicked himself. (Deut. 14:17) "Do not allow a woman to dress as a man, or vice versa," he commanded. (Deut. 22:5) This was abhorrent to God because he found it vaguely homo-ish. "Don't plant a field with an ox and an ass together; I'm not sure why, I just don't like it!" (Deut. 22:10) "Bury your poo when you squat," God finally got around to telling Moses. (Deut. 23:14) God thought his description of pooping, "squatting," was excellent. Lastly, but perhaps most importantly, if two men were fighting and one of their wives showed up and tried to help her husband by grabbing the other man's penis? (This was apparently something that was happening a great deal; people couldn't keep their hands off penises.) "Cut her hand off," God told Moses. "Cut it clean off, show no pity." (Deut. 25:11–12)

God got very into causing hemorrhoids at this time. (Deut. 28:27) "I can make peoples' anuses swell up and get itchy!" he crowed to some angels, clapping his hands together in delight. He'd tormented people in a wide variety of ways, but he'd never caused them anal discomfort before! See how they liked *that*!

God gave the Ashdods hemorrhoids, then the Ehronites, then the Philistines. (1 Sam. 5:6–12) The Ehronites *died* from their hemorrhoids, which God was quite proud of. God *loved* making people's anuses blow out; he thought it was funny every single time. God also very much enjoyed the fact that the Philistines made *golden hemorrhoids* to appease his people. (1 Sam. 6:5) "They are so traumatized by the hemorrhoids I gave them that they are making icons of them! They could have just paid my people in gold nuggets, but they decided to make golden buttholes! That is hilarious." God didn't laugh much—being the author of all reality was serious work after all—but *this* made him cry with laughter.

Almost there, God thought. Almost to the end of the story. Or to *this* part of it anyway. Not to the *whole* story, obviously; that was going to roll on and on (mostly in ways that God would not like, he knew) for thousands of years more, before he finally ended it. But it was nearly the end of this very important part of the story: God's people were just about to take their rightful place in the world. ("Why didn't I just put them there at the start?" popped into his head, but by now he was quite comfortable with retorting, "I had my reasons, whether I understood them or not.")

After Moses was gone, God did miss him. He'd been a great friend and ally. God had opened up to him in ways that he never had before. And the guy who replaced him, Joshua? Well, he was a good general, but honestly, he was *boring*. Moses had been a big personality, fun and exciting. Joshua was the sort of guy that neither God nor his angels had much interest in talking to. The one angel God sent down to visit him couldn't get out of there soon enough. "What do you wish of me?" Joshua had asked in that flat, dull voice of his, and the angel was so eager to leave that all he told Joshua to do was to take his sandals off. Which Joshua did, allowing the angel to depart. (Josh. 5:13) Everybody laughed about that for a long time.

Still, Joshua was a strong leader—"very strong on impaling," God had to admit (Josh. 8:29, 10:26)—and he led his people toward Canaan. At one point, to help him out a little bit, God stopped the sun. (Josh 10:13–14) Needless to say, this was something he could have done anytime he wanted to. He'd just never *wanted* to before. "And I never will again," he whispered to himself, out of breath. Although God acted like it was easy, stopping the sun was actually fairly difficult. It worked, though. Not long after he did it, victory was achieved. "Everything is fulfilled," God told his angels triumphantly. (Josh. 21:43)

It *felt* true at that moment, it really did. But oh, those impossible humans. Even in the midst of success, they *still* doubted, they *still* drifted toward Baal. Outraged, God hammered them again and again until, before long, they were living in caves again. (Jud. 6:2) God felt disconcerted by this sudden fall—and even more so after the "Jephthah debacle," as he called it.

Here's what happened: A man named Jephthah was leading God's people and, at a key moment, he made the following deal with God: "If you help me defeat the Ammonites, I will kill whoever walks out of my front door." (Jud. 11:30) God agreed to the deal, then winced when Jephthah's teenage daughter emerged through the door. It was something like the Abraham and Isaac situation, except that in *this* case, God did not send down an angel to stop Jephthah, who actually did kill his daughter. "Who did he think would walk out of his own house?" God asked, feeling slightly queasy as he watched Jephthah strangle the crying, terrified girl.

"I'm glad I don't know her name," God muttered, watching the poor girl die. "What kind of God *am I*?" he briefly wondered. "That I allow this man to slaughter his daughter for me when I can stop the sun without asking for any sacrifice at all?" God silently stared down at Jephthah's daughter's lifeless body for a long moment, then turned away.

Chapter Fifteen

And then, somewhat amazingly, things suddenly got dramatically better. (Maybe the sacrifice of that girl *did* work?) A series of men came along who God liked very much indeed. First came Samson. "He ate honey out of a lion's skeleton!" God cried happily, not exactly sure why he liked this so much. (Jud. 14:9) "He killed a thousand people with a donkey's jawbone!" (Jud. 15:15) "He had super-powered hair! He was a good dancer!" In time, Samson fell in love with a conniving little bitch named Delilah and had his eyes gouged out. But damn, he was fun to watch!

After Samson, God fell for an extremely handsome young man named Saul. Saul became king and God had very positive feelings about him—for awhile. Then, and he wasn't quite sure why, God started to feel rather differently about Saul. There was something indecisive about Saul, maybe that was it. He was the sort of man who would say he was going to kill his son, for instance, and then not do it! (1 Sam 14:44–45) God didn't much like that. He started ignoring Saul at times; he began to regret that he'd made him king. "I will send an evil spirit to scare him!" God decided. (1 Sam. 16:14) ("Does this mean that 'evil' can come directly from *me*?" God wondered, stroking his chin. "Not at all, I am pure good.")

Saul brought in a musician to help him drown out the evil spirit's voice. That musician was named David and—well, what can you say about this remarkable young man? David was so very clever and quick—not to mention being a beautiful boy!

Saul's son, Jonathan (the one he should have killed), fell in love with David (1 Sam. 18:1), and God understood that in a way; David was gorgeous and charming, but he was furious about it too. Homosexuality was abhorrent. Jonathan would have to die. (As for David—well, everyone loved him and he loved everyone, and how could you hold that *against* him? Lovely boy.)

Saul soon became jealous of David and, due to that evil spirit God had put in him, tried to kill the boy. (1 Sam. 18:11) God pretty much *hated* Saul now. He allowed the evil spirit to drive Saul crazy. Before long he was stripping naked (unacceptable!) and talking gibberish. (1 Sam. 19:24) Saul went back and forth, wanting to kill David, then begging his forgiveness. He was falling apart, clearly driven mad by the fact that God wouldn't even talk to him anymore.

God was infuriated when Saul talked to the ghost of the previous leader, Samuel. The idea of this conversation was maddening—but what Samuel's ghost actually said was correct. "God hates you, Saul, and I'll tell you why: Because you didn't wipe out the Amalekites!" (This was true. God hadn't forgotten those bastards. Bizarrely, the Amalekites were doing very well considering how much the creator of reality—him!—despised them and had vowed their annihilation.)

Saul was killed soon after that and good riddance. (That awful homosexual son of his, Jonathan, died at the same time.) God couldn't help but nod approvingly when he saw the Philistines cut Saul's head off and impale his dead body. (1 Sam. 31:9–10) "Karma," he muttered to himself, before remembering that karma didn't exist and was a completely made-up idea.

God didn't much like David's eulogy to Jonathan: "Your love was wonderful to me, more than the love of women?" he snorted. (2 Sam. 1:26) But he let it pass. He liked David that much and come on, you could hardly say the guy didn't like women! ("I certainly am tolerant of those few people I like, though, aren't

I?" God mused to himself.) After David became king, he banned the lame and the blind from the temple because he hated them. (2 Sam. 5:8) God agreed wholeheartedly. The lame and the blind disgusted him.

Like Samson, actually even more so, David was a terrific dancer. God loved men who could dance. "I like to watch them move," he thought to himself. It was hard to overstate just how much God loved David. He frankly *adored* this beautiful, delightful, charming man, and he gave him everything he wanted, spoiling him like an indulgent parent would. At last, the son he had always wanted!

David did do things that God knew were wrong. Sending your mistress's husband into battle to be killed? (2 Sam. 11:15) God scolded David for this. But when David apologized, God quickly forgave him and gave him a son who would be, astoundingly, even more clever than he was!

Solomon was a brilliant fellow. He had the most complex and interesting mind God had ever encountered in a person. God gave Solomon a kind of wisdom and discernment he had never handed out before and never would again. (1 K. 3:12) This was a very positive thing overall; the kingdom thrived. There was great wealth, the people were happy, there was a navy, for goodness' sake! (1 K. 9:26) But (and wasn't there always, always a "but" when it came to humans?) sometimes God wondered whether he had given Solomon a bit *too much* wisdom.

Solomon wrote a lot, you see; he was quite prolific. There was a lot of what he wrote that God heartily approved of. "Trust in the Lord with all your heart," for instance—or "Fear the Lord and shun evil." "Honor the Lord with your wealth" was also good. (Prov. 3:5–9) But there were other things that Solomon wrote that God almost couldn't believe he was seeing.

Solomon wrote a poem to one of his girlfriends that literally made God *blush* when he read it. "What is THIS doing in my book?" God demanded. A few angels tried to tell God that Solomon's love poem was written to him, not to the woman, but God shook his head dismissively. "I don't think Solomon is telling *me* that my breasts are like fawns. (Song 7:4) He better not be!" One angel with a weird, slightly shifty look that bothered God suggested that perhaps Solomon was writing *as* God, complimenting mankind's "rounded thighs." (Song 7:2) God had this angel killed.

But this love poem was nothing compared to another piece that Solomon wrote, a piece that more or less contradicted the rest of God's entire book. (Solomon claimed his brother, "Koheleth," wrote it, but come on, it was him.) It was called "Ecclesiastes" and it made God's jaw drop. "'The meaning of life is to eat, drink, and be *merry*'? (Ecc. 2:24, 3:12, 11:9) NONSENSE!" God roared. "The meaning of life is to OBEY ME and Solomon *knows* that!" And saying that a human's life was no more meaningful than a goat's—or even a worm's? (Ecc. 3:18–19) Ludicrous. Why not just say, "Everything you've read up to this point is worthless nonsense?" God could not fathom why Solomon was writing such craziness. One (supposedly) wise old man later suggested that "it was actually kind of profound, Lord." God literally ripped that old man's head off and kicked it down to hell.

(And let's not even get started on that other thing that Solomon wrote—pertaining to the very events that God didn't want to think about and had vowed not to and—no—no—no more about that.)

But in the end, it wasn't Solomon's writings that were the real problem. The real problem was that the man was, to put it very crudely, an insatiable pussy hound. And honestly, even *that* wasn't the real problem. No, the real problem was this: Solomon loved all women—including non-Hebrew women. In fact, he loved some of these non-Hebrew women enough that he allowed them to talk to him about their own nonexistent gods! Solomon would listen to them—he would even flirt with those fake gods! Solomon, God's greatest man, the one who had finally realized his plans, and even *he* couldn't be counted on! (1 K. 11:1–8) "I have led them to the pinnacle of success and *this* is how they reward me? What is *wrong* with these people??"

("And what is wrong with me that I picked them?" came the dark response. "They were the only ones who believed in me, I had no choice!" he found himself responding—but that didn't make him feel better.)

Once Solomon flamed out, it was a sudden and steep fall for God's people. Things went from bad to worse for them—"exactly as they deserved," God said indignantly. There were struggles for power, civil wars, military defeats, and lots of poor leaders. God was in a bad mood now and at times he lashed out in ways that he would wonder about for a moment, before he reassured himself of his own perfect judgment. The incident with Elisha and the bears, for example, was, well—slightly embarrassing. At the time, God was feeling irritable and it felt like the right thing to do—but was it?

Elisha was a prophet, as his father Elijah had been before him. Elijah had killed a *lot* of Baal's followers, and God appreciated that. (1 K. 18:40) So much so that he sent a fire-chariot drawn by fire-horses down from heaven to pick Elijah up when he died. (2 K. 2:11) The only problem with Elijah was that he was extremely hairy. God didn't like hairy men. Elisha was less hairy; he was bald, in fact, with a gleaming, hairless head. One day, as Elisha was going from town to town, prophesying, some boys saw him coming and shouted, "Go away, baldhead!" at him. God, looking down at this, was instantly enraged. How *dare* those children yell at his shiny-headed prophet? He thought about fire-blasting them from heaven or turning them all to salt, but he had a better idea: God quickly sent two she-bears to maul the children. The bears killed forty-two children. (2 K. 2:23–24)

"The children were teasing Elisha for being bald?" Satan asked, the next time they met.

"That's right."

"And you had them all mauled by bears for that?"

God's jaw was tight, he hated this kind of questioning. "*Correct.*"

"How many children were actually yelling, God? Two? Three?"

"At least five."

"Why did the other thirty-seven children get mauled?"

"They were *present*, Satan, that was enough."

Satan smiled, his small, dark eyes glittering. "Your justice, as always, is perfect, God."

He was being sarcastic, but God didn't take the bait. "Thank you, Satan. Coming from *you*, that means a lot."

"I think it probably does mean a lot, yes."

And it did mean a lot. Damn it, it did.

Fine, maybe he could have killed fewer children, like fifteen or twenty. Maybe killing forty-two children *was* a bit excessive. On the other hand, God told himself, it was quite likely that many of the children had been disobedient at some point and therefore deserved to be killed. Also, some of them were undoubtedly homosexual, so they deserved death. At least one or two had probably had sex with a goat or a sheep, so *they* had it coming too. Overall, when he thought about it, probably most of the children deserved to die. Also, God couldn't help but feel somewhat proud of how he had so quickly "possessed" the two she-bears and used them to mangle the children. "I can puppet bears!" he'd noted to himself. "That is fantastic."

God also briefly cheered himself up with the way he killed that Baal-loving harlot, Jezebel. He had her thrown off a building, then trampled by horses, then eaten by dogs! (2 K. 9:33–37) ("I hate women so much," God found himself murmuring under his breath, as he watched the dogs tear Jezebel's bloody carcass apart.)

Not long after that, God killed 185,000 Assyrians in one day. (2 Kings 19:35) He hadn't killed that many people in a long time, and it felt great. Still, it puzzled him. "I can stop the sun, I can kill 185,000 people, I can control people's—and *bear's*—minds . . . but my people are circling the drain! Why is that? Also—why don't the Assyrians even seem to *acknowledge* that I just killed 185,000 of them, what is *that* about?!"

Chapter Sixteen

That was the beginning of the dark times.

Things went horribly for God's people for a very long time and, frankly, God didn't much care. He was feeling more and more finished with his people. He didn't want to help them anymore; what he wanted to do was berate them and tell them how wicked they were for several hundred years. He used his prophets to do this.

Isaiah came first. There were things God liked about him. The part about God's enemies' babies being dashed to pieces on rocks was excellent. (Isa. 13:16) Also good was when Isaiah talked about how God had killed all of the other gods. (Isa. 26:13–14) ("Fine, they did exist the whole time, whatever. I had my reasons," God thought curtly to himself, then smiled, remembering the other gods screaming as they were mauled by she-bears.) God also liked the way Isaiah capitalized every version of his name. "There is no anger in Me," Isaiah had God saying, for example. "Isaiah's *right*! I am so great that all descriptions of Me should be capitalized!" God exclaimed. He also appreciated that Isaiah correctly perceived that there was no anger in Him. Anyone opposed to Him *would* be set on fire, that was true. (Isa. 27:4) But not out of anger. No. Out of righteousness. Ultimately, however, God thought Isaiah was a bore. He talked way too much for way too long, and God was glad when he died.

Jeremiah, who came next, was even worse. He was duplicitous—pretty obviously using God to curry favor with the King of Babylon, Nebuchadnezzar. Even his own people saw through Jeremiah, locking him up for telling them to surrender to Nebuchadnezzar again and again. (Jere. 38:6) What Jeremiah did, however, make clear was how very much God hated his people by this time. They were stupid and unintelligent. (Jere. 4:22) They were, let's be blunt, firewood. (Jere. 5:14) Yes, it was sad but true; God had decided to burn his own people like firewood, that's how much they mattered to him. They had hurt his feelings too many times. He loathed them by this point and he told them so: "I come to loathe you," he said. "You are dung and I will make an end of you." (Jere. 8:2) It had gotten that bad; God's people were shit to him and he would wipe them out. He didn't *care* what people would say about him anymore—didn't care about his fame or reputation or anything. It was time to end this thing and start over—*right now.*

And then—and God couldn't really understand this—for some reason, he didn't end it. When God looked back on this period of time much later, it seemed a blur to him. Things were going badly, his people were losing, he was furious with them, even *more* furious at their enemies—but strangely ineffective at *changing* anything.

"I am all powerful, yet nothing ever seems to go the way I want it to. That's bizarre," God thought to himself.

He kept complaining about his people. "I am shattered, dejected, seized with desolation," he told Jeremiah (Jere. 8:21)—which afterward, he felt a little bit weird about. "I made up this game, how can I be *losing* it?" Why *didn't* he just end this whole thing and start over? He honestly wasn't sure anymore.

"It's all a conspiracy," God found himself saying to Jeremiah at one point, and instantly wished he hadn't. (Jere. 11:9) "Only weak, paranoid people think there are conspiracies against them, right?" God asked the nearest angel. The angel shook his head and said no no, of course not, it sounded commanding and strong, just like everything you say, blah blah blah.

But God didn't trust his angels anymore. They were a bunch of sycophants. The only one who ever told him the truth, as much as he hated to admit it, was Satan. But he knew what he would say: "Maybe you're not wiping them all out because you *can't*, God." Which was absurd—*obviously*. So God didn't ask Satan for his opinion, because he knew beforehand how wrong and misguided it would be.

Enough. No more talk.

God was going to *act*, he was *done*, and this time he meant it. "I am abandoning you, deserting you," he told Jeremiah. (Jere. 12:7) It was over. He was leaving, not even bothering to kill everyone, not even caring enough to do it anymore—he was going and he was *not* coming back. God started to leave, feeling determined and clear-headed. "This is good," he thought to himself, happy to be done with his people, happy to be on the way out.

It was strange though . . . no matter how many times he said he was done, God found himself continuing to talk to Jeremiah, venting about how much he hated his people. "I will exterminate them, I will destroy them, etc." (Jere. 14:12, 15:7) He didn't do it though. He didn't leave, he didn't destroy his people, he didn't do much of anything except keep yelling about how mad he was. God had long ago accepted that his plan was mysterious, but this was baffling. "What am I doing?" he thought to himself. "I'm making a fool of myself here! I *have* to leave now. I *have* to stop talking and *go* right now!!"

"Dogs will drag your carcasses through the streets and buzzards will eat your guts," God screamed at Jeremiah (Jere. 15:3), thinking, as he did: Stop talking, God. STOP.

Not long after that, Nebuchadnezzar attacked Jerusalem. God was stunned and furious about this. (Jere. 51:34) Nebuchadnezzar and his whore of a city (for Babylon was the most whorish city God had ever seen!) would be annihilated. It would be worse than Sodom and Gomorrah! "I will club children to death!"

God growled, eager for his bloody vengeance. (Jere. 51:22) God rubbed his hands together, prepared to obliterate Babylon. "Run away," he told his people, "I'm just about to do it."

And then . . . and then . . .

He didn't do anything. Babylon burned Jerusalem to the ground, looted it, stripped it bare—and God didn't do a thing. (Jere. 52) He just sat in heaven and watched it happen, silent and motionless.

Chapter Seventeen

God felt confused and conflicted, sometimes immobilized with uncertainty and doubt at this time. He couldn't help but notice that as things went from bad to worse, his prophets became less and less appealing as people. David and Solomon—now they were men! These days he was dealing with the likes of Isaiah ("a windy bore"), Jeremiah ("a schemer, playing all the angles")—and now, ugh, the worst one yet: Ezekiel.

"This guy is a freak," God thought to himself as soon as he and Ezekiel started working together. God wanted to test Ezekiel, see just how crazy he was, so he told him to eat a scroll, which Ezekiel promptly did. (Ezek. 3:1) God then tested him again, telling him to eat poop, which Ezekiel also did. (Ezek. 4:12) Finally, God told Ezekiel to shave his beard and divide the hairs into three equal parts, burning a third, attacking a third with a sword, and scattering the final third in the wind. Also, God told him, save a few hairs and sew them up in your shirt. "He'll never do all that," God told himself. "He's not that loony." But of course, he was. Ezekiel did everything God told him to. (Ezek. 5:1–4) God was stuck with him.

And it wasn't just that Ezekiel was insane. He was also, to be honest, a creep. He started claiming that God was saying things that God would *never* actually say, like talking about Jerusalem as a young woman and referring to her firm breasts and pubic hair. "I saw that your time for love had arrived," Ezekiel had God saying to Jerusalem, implying that he wanted to have sex with the city! (Ezek. 16:7–8) Which was outrageous! God had made it *abundantly* clear, over and over, that sex was *not* something he approved of. (Also, God had very little interest in breasts.)

But Ezekiel didn't stop. He kept talking about perverted things. He brought up how God's people had taken all the gold and silver God had given them and melted it down into . . . well . . . "phallic items," shall we say? (Ezek. 16:17) ("You mean dildos?" Satan had later chuckled, vulgar as always.) This was true, they had done that and God had been incensed about it, no doubt—but it was crass to talk about it.

God wanted Ezekiel to shut up. The guy kind of repulsed him—he was so *warped*. God thought of killing him but the truth was, he didn't have a lot of great men to choose from at this time; he couldn't honestly be sure that the next guy would be any better. So God let Ezekiel live.

But he sometimes regretted it. Ezekiel wouldn't stop with the sex stories. Now he started saying God was talking about young women with "virgin nipples" who lusted after men whose "organs were like those of stallions." (Ezek. 23:8–21) This was ridiculous! *One* time, God had referred to a certain angel that way—*once*. It was not something he was in the habit of saying!

God didn't like Ezekiel, who he felt was making him look bad. He wasn't sure what to do—so he decided to bring some skeletons to life. (Ezek. 37:5) That helped for a moment, but not for long. Finally, Ezekiel died and a bunch of minor prophets came along. None of them was very interesting to God; he didn't talk to them much and when he did, he didn't say much of interest: "You're whores—ruled by your dicks—drunks— lechers—I'm done with you and this time I mean it blah blah blah!" God was depressed during this time. He drank a lot of wine, ate a lot of veal, gained weight. He continued to think about wiping everything out and starting over, but by this time he had serious doubts as to whether he would actually do it.

At certain moments, the answer to God's problem seemed obvious to him: Why not *make* his people love and obey him? Why not make *everyone* love and obey him? He could do that, obviously. Why didn't he? Everyone would be happier. Maybe he'd had some limited hope that people would choose to love and obey him, but that was quite obviously not going to happen. He should just fix things, that's what he should do. Fine, God concluded. I will accept that my creation was flawed and I will fix it. I will do it . . . right . . . *now*!

But once again, he just sat there.

Time passed. God considered bringing more skeletons to life, then decided that was pointless. He felt angry again. He was God. He didn't have to explain or justify himself to anyone. He'd made the Sun, dammit! The idea that humans, lowly worms that they were, would question or doubt him was enraging. He decided, instead of fixing things, to throw shit in their faces. (Mal. 2:3) *That's* what they deserved. He didn't actually go through with it, mainly because he disliked shit so much that he didn't want to handle it—but he wanted to do it, he really did.

There was *one* moment—looking back, God didn't really understand it—when he felt and behaved quite differently. "Jonah seemed to bring out the best in me for some reason," God noted. "To start with, I wanted him to *convert* people, which I don't remember wanting at any other time back then. For another, when Jonah didn't want to do it, rather than punishing him, which I ordinarily would have done, I taught him a lesson in a, let's say, whimsical way. Finally, when he wanted his converts, the Ninevans (who I normally detested) to be punished, I said no. I told him I wanted to reach people, not hurt them, I didn't even want to hurt their animals." (Jon. 2:1, 4:11) Honestly, God had no idea what had come over him at this time. Maybe it had something to do with those odd mushrooms one of his angels had gathered on earth and given to him? "After I ate them, I have to admit that I felt calmer, less angry—like somehow I was part of something bigger than myself. It was beautiful." That feeling passed, of course, and when it did, God found himself even angrier than he'd been before.

When God looked back at this overall period, much later, he felt that it was the lowpoint of his career. "I wanted to throw poo in my own people's faces, you know?" he said to that stallion-hung angel. "How much worse can it get than *that*? You know?"

Slowly, inexorably, something was building inside God—something dark and troubling. He fought it with everything he could, tried to hold it in, but he simply couldn't do it.

One day, talking to—or technically, shrieking at—Hosea, he heard his voice catch. "I loved you and you forgot me," he wailed. (Hos. 11:1–7) Another time, talking to Micah, he heard his shuddering voice cry out, "What wrong have I done you?" (Micah 6:3) He felt wetness on his cheeks—something salty—what was happening to him?

Suddenly, it was clear. All God had ever wanted was *love*. Why didn't people love him? Why did they love others instead? No one loved him, no one ever had. He had never been touched, God suddenly realized; never been held or comforted in any way—and the knowledge of that was suffocating and heavy and almost unbearably sad.

God found himself sobbing, his body shaking with rage and pain, anguished at the (literal) infinity of loneliness he had known. No mother, no father, no siblings, no friends. Nothing. He was alone. He had always been alone.

It was time, he knew, to look at that unfortunate series of events that had happened so long before, the ones that he had blocked out, that he had told himself a hundred, no a thousand times, were meaningless—but which he now understood to have been extremely important.

It was time, he knew, to look back.

Chapter Eighteen

Sometime long before, after the Tower of Babel but before Sodom and Gomorrah, there had been a man named Job who loved God very much. God liked that about him. It made God feel wonderful that this good man—for Job was a good man, a blameless man, really (Job 1:1)—loved him so faithfully.

God was throwing a lot of parties at this time; he'd just started working on heaven and he liked to walk angels around and show them how amazing it was going to be. Sometimes he would invite 10–15 angels and they would all listen, rapt, as God discussed his stunning achievements, how he had literally created everything in the universe in a single week. Sometimes the angels would spontaneously applaud God, and while he didn't expect or demand it, he did enjoy it. But the main thing God liked to talk about at this time was Job. God never got tired of telling everyone how much this flawless man loved him.

And then, at a certain party, Satan showed up. (Job 1:6) He was not invited, obviously. He was not supposed to be in heaven at all, except for occasional and brief meetings about hell. But there he was. God and Satan had had limited interactions since the whole tree of knowledge thing. God didn't like the way Satan had handled it and he *strongly* disliked how insinuating and, at times, frankly, disrespectful Satan had been toward him. So what was he doing here at God's garden party? Did he show up just to ruin it, because he hated, resented, and was jealous of God (which he obviously was)? God didn't want to get upset in front of his angels, so he didn't do what in hindsight he obviously should have done, which was to kick Satan out. Instead, he tried to stay calm as if, yes, of *course* he'd invited Satan to his party. It's not like he snuck into heaven.

There was a strained pause. The angels looked at Satan, then back at God. Everyone knew these two didn't like each other. Satan stood there, not saying anything, an annoyingly blank look on his face. God was going to stare right back at him, stare him down, he had no problem with that—but then he decided to take the high road, be a good host, actually engage Satan in a friendly conversation. "Where have you been?" he asked. (Job 1:7) Not that he didn't know the answer to this, obviously. He always knew the answer, every single time he asked a question. He was just being polite.

"I have been roaming the earth," Satan answered, and for a moment God thought about saying, "Why weren't you working on hell, *that's* your job?" But he decided not to. Glancing over at his angels, God nodded grandly and said, "Did you see Job? He's a very good man who loves me and hates evil" (Job 1:8) (Meaning: "He loves me and hates you, Satan. Suck on *that*.")

Satan's response was quick: "Why wouldn't he love you? He has a nice life. Take that life away from him and see if he still loves you then." (Job 1:9–11) God felt his entire body tense up. Satan was publicly challenging him. "He snuck into my party and then, when I tried to make polite small talk with him, he attacked me. I should kill him right now."

But God decided that it would look weak if he reacted violently against Satan. "No, I will act as if I am amused by what he is saying," he told himself. He smiled broadly, shrugged, and in the most supremely confident voice he could affect (which was *very* supremely confident, he felt), he said: "Go ahead then, Satan, ruin his life, I don't care, just don't physically hurt him." (Job 1:12)

Satan looked at God for a moment, then nodded and walked away without saying another word. Instantly, God regretted what he'd said. He liked Job very much and now he'd given Satan— *Satan*—permission to destroy the man's life. "Why didn't I say something like 'Think whatever you like, Satan, you obviously are trying to goad me into giving you permission to torture Job, but guess what, I'm not going to give it to you. By the way, you weren't invited to this party and I'd like you to leave!'"

God watched in disbelief as, in a matter of hours, Satan dismantled his faithful servant's life: Job's cows and camels were stolen, his sheep were burned up by holy fire ("unnecessarily harsh," God muttered to himself), his servants were killed, and then, in one fell swoop, all of his children were crushed in a freak windstorm. (Job 1:13–19) God did have to admire Satan's skill, much as he disliked what was happening. "Killing ten people in one house in a windstorm is not easy," he noted to himself. (It took him fourteen tries to do it to some Amalekites a bit later.)

Still, guess what? Good news. The point that God had wanted to make? Well, it was made. *Job was still faithful.* (Job 1:22) God knew he would be, of course, but it felt good to be so publicly vindicated. "It will be interesting to hear what Satan has to say *now,*" God chortled. "I imagine he will be singing a slightly different tune the next time I see him." God felt so good that he decided to throw another party. ("Given all of my responsibilities, do I throw too many parties?" he'd asked himself, then quickly answered: "No, I enjoy throwing parties and that is that.")

Satan showed up again. God smiled as he saw him approach, looking forward to hearing his nemesis eat his words. "Oh Satan—where have you been?" God asked, goading him. (Job 2:2) When Satan didn't even respond, God decided to let him have it: "You see, Satan, you were *wrong.* Job still loves me, even though you incited me to destroy him for no good reason." (Job 2:3) God quickly stopped, thinking about what he'd just said. Had he just admitted that there was no good reason for Job's life to be ruined? He had, yes. That wasn't a smart thing to say, he felt. He was God; God was supposed to have good reasons—perfect reasons—for everything he did. He thought about correcting himself: "What I meant to say, of course, was that you incited me against Job exactly as I wished you to, in order to prove my point, Satan." But he decided not to, thinking that it sounded somewhat convoluted.

Satan, that bastard, retorted with, "He still loves you, God, only because he's not in physical pain. Let me cause him bodily pain and *then* see what happens." (Job 2:5) God was incensed by this. He'd won the wager, but rather than acknowledging it, Satan was challenging him again. He was not going to let Satan know he was annoyed, however. God feigned his most superior smile and shrugged: "Go ahead then, do whatever you want, just don't kill him." (Job 2:6) As Satan nodded and walked away, God rolled his eyes at his angel party-guests, as if to say, can you believe this guy? But on the inside, God didn't feel great about what was happening.

Satan covered Job from head to toe with boils. It looked incredibly painful. Job's wife (what was her name? . . . oh, who cares?) was still alive. God couldn't help but chuckle at Satan's nasty joke: Job was worse off with his wife alive than dead, *ha*, exactly right! She told him that he should curse God. (Job 2:9) ("I'm going to get her for that," God muttered to himself. "She *did* just lose ten children," flickered across his mind but he dismissed it, mumbling "whore" to himself as he did.) Job, though, bless his soul, stayed strong and loyal to God. "One must accept the evil as well as the good," he responded. (Job 2:10)

Even though God felt a little bit guilty about the way he'd let his favorite man's life be ruined, he felt great about being vindicated for a second time. Satan had said that Job would not love him if he was in pain, and he had been proven *completely wrong*. God was right. Job still loved him. God realized later that he should have called the wager over at that very moment. "I won, Satan," he should have said.

Because the truth was, not long afterward, God's glorious victory started to crumble.

Job sat on the ground, mourning his existence, regretting that he'd ever been born. (Job 3:3) Hearing this, God seethed. Obedient, loving Job was suddenly and not-so-subtly criticizing him! When Job said that God had "hedged him around" (Job 3:23), God's insides churned.

"Hedged him around? What does that even *mean*?" he boomed. On some level, of course, he knew exactly what it meant, and it wasn't good. The wager—"Job will be faithful to me no matter what"—that he had so clearly won? Well, it began to look as if . . . hard to even acknowledge this . . . Satan had perhaps been at least partially right.

Satan didn't show up to claim victory, which God was thankful for. God decided to wait and see what would happen next. (He knew what was going to happen, needless to say: He was going to lose the bet more and more embarrassingly until, in the end, he was going to make a colossal fool of himself in an event that would haunt him for thousands of years to come.)

Chapter Nineteen

Job's friends showed up. God was hoping that they would argue on his behalf, but when they *did*, they were, to be blunt, such monumental dicks that he wished they hadn't. Zophar, Bildud, and Eliphaz traveled a distance to see their friend Job and, at first, they wept. (Job 2:12) "Fakes!" God practically yelled down at them. "It's obvious you're happy about what's happened to Job!"

These three guys spent the next several days hectoring Job: "You must have done something wrong; Your children must have deserved it; You deserved worse than this," things like that. God almost couldn't believe what shitheads these three friends were. So much so that when they kept pointing out how great and wondrous and just God was (Job 5:9, 8:3), he shook his head and muttered, "I wish they'd shut up."

But they didn't shut up, they kept yammering on and on. And the more they talked, the worse God felt. Because the more Job responded to them, the worse things he said: "God is terrorizing me." (Job 6:4) "I wish he'd just kill me." (Job 6:9) God bristled. Maybe Job *did* have this coming. And it got even worse. Before long, Job was talking about suing God! (Job 9:2–4) "Even though I'm good," Job said, "God would prove me bad. God mocks the innocent as they suffer." (Job 9:23) ("The mocking part was untrue," Satan would later say. "You don't mock, God, because you have absolutely no sense of humor.")

As to the wager, why was it continuing? "I suppose I could end it now," God thought—"but then I'd have to admit I lost." An eternity of Satan gloating about his win? That was *not* going to happen. Satan was going to pay for letting the bet continue. At some point, Job was going to come back around and when he did, at *that* moment, God would end the bet, thus outsmarting Satan!

The one thing that God could cling onto was that Job had not, technically speaking, "blasphemed" him, so in *that* sense, he had not yet lost the wager. "But the only reason he's not blaspheming me to my face is that I'm not there!" God's nostrils flared as Job kept trashing him. "God is defrauding me" (Job 10:3); "God is a liar" (Job 10:7); "God is a bully" (Job 10:16); "I wish God would leave me alone." (Job 10:20) God wanted to attack Job at that moment, kill him and send him to proto-hell. But he continued to restrain himself: How would it look to kill his favorite human, whose very faithfulness he had wagered on, in front of his angels?

God looked around, suddenly nervous. Where was Satan? Why *wasn't* he claiming his victory? Job was attacking him. Satan had won. It would be hard to argue that he hadn't, yet he was nowhere to be seen. Why would he be so foolish as to let the wager continue? Was he up to something? God suddenly felt very anxious.

After all three friends had spoken, God relaxed ever so slightly for a moment, hoping that perhaps the hideous, humiliating back and forth between them and Job was over. "Maybe things'll get a bit better," God hoped to himself (knowing that they wouldn't; knowing in his guts that he loathed himself and had created this entire machine to punish himself for his bottomless, eternal, infernal wickedness.)

Job went after God yet again, demanding that he "take his hands off him," as if he wanted to *fight him*. (Job 13:21) God trembled with rage. "Where are you, God, why don't you show yourself?" Job demanded, essentially challenging God. (Job

13:24) "I'll tear him apart, limb by limb!" God blurted—then looked around to see if anyone had heard him. He saw some angels a ways off and . . . wait . . . was that Satan? Was he here to end the wager? God wanted it to end now; this situation was rapidly becoming a complete debacle.

But it wasn't Satan. The wager rolled on. God shook his head, no no no, as the three friends started to hold forth *again*, telling Job that he was sinful, loathsome, and foul. (Job 15:5, 18:5) God, furious as he was, couldn't help but snicker. "With friends like those . . ." He was enraged at Job for his insolence, but these friends were just such monumental pricks! "You're the evil ones," Job retorted (Job 19:29), before he started weeping. *Now* it will end, God told himself.

But of course it didn't. The friends started saying things that were simply idiotic: "You will die like your shit" (Job 20:7); "Food will turn to snake venom in your belly" (Job 20:14); "Anything that doesn't turn to venom, you will puke back up." (Job 20:15) They were making things up! None of this was true! Job was being punished for "torturing the poor," they said (Job 20:19), and God rolled his eyes. These guys were *unbelievably* horrible friends. They just kept topping themselves in the idiot department! "You're like a worm," they told Job, "you're like a maggot." (Job 25:6) (On some level, of course, this was basically true. Since God was pure good, all the evil in the world *had* to have come from mankind. The only thing that sometimes seemed odd: How had he created such vile worms in his own image?)

Job was silent for a moment. Maybe it was over now? God prayed. Then Job spoke again: "God is cruel, our pain means nothing to him, less than nothing." (Job 30:19–21) *"Not true!"* God thought. "I care deeply about my creations. Their pain affects me . . . you know . . . a lot . . ." He trailed off, knowing this wasn't true. He *didn't* care, it was obvious; he'd just allowed the destruction of his favorite man's life on a party bet. How could he claim to care?

The wager had blown up in God's face, humiliating him in front of all his angels; he wanted it *over* at this point. But Satan still did not show up to claim his victory. Why was he allowing the bet to go on and on? "Because every minute that goes by is worse for you," popped into his head. "Because he knows you and understands your vanity and pride and is using them to make a complete fool of you."

"*Wrong*," God shouted internally. "*Wrong wrong wrong!*" No one was making a fool of *him*! If Satan's plan was to draw the bet out to make God look bad (and by the way, it probably *wasn't*, that was probably giving Satan way too much credit; he was probably working on hell, *that's* probably what he was doing), if he was "scheming," well, God knew how to throw it right back in his damned evil face!

"I will send another man into the conversation!" God exulted. "This young man will argue on my behalf with eloquence and passion. He will silence all the others and, yes, *shame* them. He will tell Job the truth about me and my greatness. After he speaks, Job will love and respect me again and I will win the bet!" It was a marvelous plan and it would work, God knew it would.

The only problem was that the young man God picked to be his advocate, Elihu? Well, let's just say he wasn't everything God might have wished for. He talked a lot, definitely—but he was annoyingly pompous and self-important. "What I'm about to tell you is quite important," he kept saying, and God squirmed. (Job 32:18, 33:3) "Get to the point!" he practically yelled. But when Elihu finally *did* get around to making God's case, well, even then God wasn't pleased. "He doesn't make it sound any better or more convincing than the other guys," God fumed.

"I'm going to have to do this myself," God began to understand. "None of them is arguing my position correctly, I will have to do it." He prepared himself to do so—then had to wait as Elihu blathered on and on. "I will teach you wisdom," he said (Job 33:33), and God considered fire-blasting him from the sky at that moment. "Don't tell people how wise you are, idiot!"

he whispered harshly. He wished the other four men would kill Elihu, stone him, impale him, anything to shut him up. It had been a huge mistake to send this little twerp in his place. Elihu was insufferable; the other men obviously hated him and God understood why. "Shut up," he began to murmur, "shut up, shut up, shut up."

But Elihu didn't shut up. "A man of sound opinion is before you," he yammered, and God shook his head in amazement. (Job 36:4) "I think he may be the single most irritating person I have ever created," God said, "and that is saying *a lot.*" God could practically feel Satan's amusement by now. He felt hot, flushed, foolish. He knew that he had to step in and fix things, quickly.

Finally, Elihu finished. There was silence. "This is the moment," God thought. "This is my time." He began to speak extremely loudly and forcefully. God had a huge, deep, powerful voice, but heaven was quite a distance from earth, so he had to yell.

Chapter Twenty

This was *not* how God had imagined the wager playing itself out, but what needed to be done needed to be done. God needed to straighten everybody out, and he was going to do so. Fine, he hadn't planned on this, he didn't have "prepared remarks," but so what? He would speak extemporaneously. "The first thing I will do is put Job in his place," God thought to himself. "How dare you question me? Did *you* make the earth?!" he bellowed. (Job 38:4) That felt good.

"Not only did I make the earth," he continued, "I made it so well that my angels shouted for joy!" (Job 38:7) Which was true; they *had* shouted for joy when God had created . . . wait . . . were there angels present when he had made the earth? No, there weren't, this was a bad start. Also, was he bragging? Did he sound insecure? Should he stop right now? Was he about to go off a cliff? These questions flashed across God's mind, but he charged on: "There is no stopping me now!"

"I created the stars!" God thundered as the five humans gaped upward in stunned silence, obviously terrified and intimidated. "I should stop now," flitted across God's mind. "I've made my point: *Don't question me.* I should stop now." But the truth was—he was just getting started. He'd been holding these feelings of wounded pride and resentment in for a long time, he was furious about how this bet had played out—and he needed to get it all off his chest. "Have you walked along the bottom of the ocean?" God boomed (Job 38:16) and then instantly thought: "That sounded bizarre. I haven't walked along the bottom of the ocean. Why did I say that? I don't even like water, it scares me." But the words were pouring out now and would not be stopped.

"Surely you know the answers to these questions!" God yelled down at Job in a taunting voice. (Job 38:21) "Stop," he began to tell himself, "stop stop stop." But he couldn't stop; he knew that he sounded mean, that he was bullying a poor sick man who'd lost all his children—a man who had been his favorite—but he couldn't restrain himself. God felt feverish; he was literally trembling with rage. The longer he talked, the more livid he felt. And as that happened, he started to say things that he didn't really understand. "I talk to lightning and it talks back to me. 'I'm ready,' it says!" he shrieked and instantly thought: "That sounds crazy." (Job 38:35)

"Get a grip, God. You're losing it—you need to stop talking right now, you sound like a lunatic." But it was no good; he was a man possessed now; possessed by hatred, rage, and bitterness. He knew Satan was laughing at him, but it didn't matter anymore; the flood of words would not, *could not*, be stopped. "Who provides food for ravens when their young cry out for God?" he bellowed. (Job 38:41) What was he *saying*? Baby ravens didn't cry out to him, he knew that. "Caw! Caw! God!" What, did parrots cry out to him too? "Brawk! Polly wants God!" *No, ludicrous!* "Why am I talking about *unicorns* now?" God wondered. (Job 39:9) "Do I actually believe in them? What, am I going to start talking about Bigfoot next?!"

To say that this was going badly would have been a colossal understatement. It was a *disaster*. The five men were staring up at the sky with baffled and, to be totally honest, vaguely concerned looks on their faces. God had lost the wager with Satan, badly. Now he was losing a lot more; he *knew* that, but he couldn't seem to stop it from happening. "Don't get started about ostriches and horses, God," he warned himself. But it was no good. "Ostriches are idiots!" he yelled. "They are so stupid they don't even fly!" No, ostriches don't fly because they *can't* fly, I *know* that! "Horses cannot be frightened!" God thundered. The men looked up at him, confused. "Horses love battle! They say 'Aha!' because they love it so much!" (Job 39:22–25) I know *nothing* about horses, this is *completely* wrong!

Job gave him an opportunity to escape this mess. He groveled on the ground and begged for mercy. "I am nothing, God," he whimpered. (Job 40:4) "Good, I can stop now," God thought to himself. "Job has been chastised; this can and should end now." God paused for a moment—then realized he wasn't through talking. He had more to say. So Job had more or less begged for mercy . . . well, his answer was no. *No mercy!* "How dare you question me!" he found himself screaming again. "How dare you question my justice! Have you a thunder-y voice like God's?" (Job 40:9) (The third person thing sounded ridiculous, he suddenly realized. Who talked about themselves in third person? Pretentious idiots!)

God's mind was spinning; he thought he was about to pass out. He was talking very fast; he thought his voice sounded high and shrill and panicky. God wanted to stop talking, he really did—but the words continued to pour out of him, loud and frantic. He caught a glimpse of himself in a mirror. He had a mad, feverish glitter in his eyes; some angels were backing away from him. Now—oh no—God started to talk about behemoth, the sea monster, and instantly, instantly, he knew that was a terrible idea. He had found himself talking about behemoth on occasion before—usually after too much wine—and thinking back, he felt that he'd always sounded too excited and emotional.

God had given behemoth a name: Leviathan. "Does Leviathan talk to you? Could you eat him if you wanted to? Could you stuff him with metal if you wanted to? Could you catch him and make him your pet? Could you tie him up so your little girls could play with him?" (Job 40:15–31) What am I *saying*? What does any of this even mean? Though he wasn't sure why, God suddenly felt extremely protective of Leviathan. "Touch him and I'll kill you!" he screamed. (Job 40:32) I'm not making any sense, I'm flailing. This is excruciating yet I cannot stop!

God was sweating profusely now, trembling. His mouth was dry, yet spittle was flying as he yelled. He wondered if he was losing his mind—if somehow this tiny little wager with Satan was going to undo him completely. "I'm a fraud," screamed his mind. "I'm a bully and a coward and a weakling. I'm a sexually confused and frightened little man, desperate to cover that up by threatening and berating—but they see what I am, they always have, that's why they don't like me, not even the ones who do!"

God's mind searched frantically for a way out of this awfulness. Should he stop talking? No, impossible, he was in too deep now; he *had* to continue. "I can *still* win this bet," he told himself; it's not too late, I'm God, I can do anything! I will pull myself out of this by . . . hmmmn . . . yes! *Continuing to talk about Leviathan!* "Who can remove his clothes?" God howled. "Who can pry the folds of his jowls apart? Who can open the doors in his face?" (Job 41:5–6)

The five men stared upward, clearly befuddled. Those were odd questions, God knew that. The point he was trying to make was, "I can handle Leviathan, can *you?*" But the "doors-in-his-face" thing sounded bizarre. Also, Leviathan didn't wear *clothes*, obviously; he was a whale-dragon!! "I must *scare* the humans," God thought. "I can still do that and I will!"

"Leviathan can breathe fire!" (Job 41:13) "He sneezes lightning!" (Job 41:10) "He has a big neck!" (Job 41:14) God stopped, suddenly exhausted. The men were staring at the ground now, clearly embarrassed. God noticed a group of angels nearby looking at him worriedly. Something caught his eye behind them—a flash of black.

Fifty feet away, near a tree, Satan looked at him. He didn't smile; he didn't do anything. He just looked at God—who knew, at that moment, that something important had changed between them. "We weren't testing Job," suddenly crossed his mind. "We were testing me."

Satan's unwavering gaze unnerved God. He blinked and looked down at earth, where Job was begging for mercy again. God took this opportunity to attack the three friends a little. He told them they were wrong and Job was right. (Job 42:7) ("By saying they were wrong, I'm basically admitting *I* was wrong," God knew. This was a first. It felt awful and he vowed to never do it again.) God restored Job's life. Or—well, not really. He instructed Mrs. Job to get pregnant ten more times ("Have fun, bitch," he whispered to himself), and he had Job's siblings restore their brother's fortune. God didn't, in truth, give Job anything at all. (Job 42:11–13) But waving his hands around and saying that he had at least allowed for a happy-ish ending to the story and God desperately wanted that. He was, he had to admit, slightly embarrassed that he couldn't get Job's cows back. "They were only stolen. I'm the creator of the universe, I can't even track down stolen cows?" he muttered to himself. Sometimes his feebleness astounded even him.

Chapter Twenty-one

Finally reflecting back on the Job disaster, God felt that he understood a few things about himself. First, he needed a break, some time off to regain his perspective. There were troubled, destructive, sometimes even *self*-destructive parts of him that he needed to get a grip on. Second, he needed an ally, someone he could trust to run things on earth while he recovered in heaven for a while.

This ally couldn't be just anyone either. It had to be family. He needed that now. God couldn't create his own mother, obviously—even if it would have been nice to have a mother to cuddle and soothe him and tell him it was all going to be okay. ("Might some of my, hmm, ambivalence about women be related to the fact that I had no mother, or if I did, that she abandoned me in a formless void?" God wondered.) He definitely didn't want a father. *He* was the father, the one and *only* father. He certainly wasn't going to create a daughter, that was a laughable idea. Whatever it was that needed to be done, he wasn't going to trust a *girl* to do it. No, he had to have a son. Moses had been an excellent friend and David had been *like* a son, but now he would have an actual son, his own flesh and blood. A son who would work for him, who would love and cherish him, and whom he would love and cherish right back. It felt wonderful to God, just thinking about it, warm and reassuring and lovely.

But as so often seemed to be the case, for all his profound wisdom and insight, there was one subject that God never quite seemed to master: Himself.

PART II

Chapter Twenty-two

Several hundred years later, God put what he referred to as "Plan B" into effect. He considered how he wanted to bring his son—Jesus was the name he'd picked—into existence. Should he create him fully formed? That hadn't worked very well with Adam and Eve so God decided against it. Should he create a baby Jesus and raise him in heaven, then send him down to earth at the age of, say, thirty? No, he had no idea how to raise a child and—to the extent that he'd seen how human children behaved, how disobedient they often were—he didn't want to try it either.

God decided to impregnate a woman and have her raise the baby Jesus. But how to actually do it? Would he have sex with the woman? God seriously considered the possibility, but couldn't seem to find a woman who sparked his interest in that way. Also, why lie? He was inexperienced—the truth was that he had *zero* experience. He was, in other words, a virgin. And the idea of things going badly? That simply could not happen.

So God chose to artificially inseminate the woman; yes, that was a better idea. (Question: once the girl was pregnant, would she be Jesus' biological *mother*, or merely a womb to carry the young god around in? Answer: God wasn't sure and he felt it didn't matter much anyway. "But probably just a womb," he thought to himself.)

Before God inseminated Mary (for that was the girl's name),

well . . . he didn't care for that part of the process. "Onanist . . . Onanist," he found himself muttering at his own reflection. God sent an angel down to earth with, more or less, a turkey baster, and Mary was quickly impregnated.

God didn't pay attention to Mary's pregnancy, nor did he really care much about Jesus' first thirty years of life. He did hear stories, apocryphal he assumed, of the boy's behavior, how he had killed people for fun, and those made him smile indulgently and murmur, "That's my boy." (Thom. 2:8–9)

When Jesus turned thirty though, the wheels started turning. Jesus started to preach God's truth. He quickly gained followers. The boy was smart and charismatic, quite a unique personality. If he lived a hundred years, he might attract followers all over the world. Or why not allow him to live *nine hundred years*, like Methuselah? Let him travel the globe, spreading the word everywhere! "Great idea, Lord," God thought to himself.

At this point, however, a question began to insinuate itself into God's mind: Given the seriousness of the job he was giving Jesus, did he fully *trust* him? Sure, he was his *son*—but given that he didn't actually "know" this young man, they'd never met obviously, and given how much was riding on him, God felt that he needed to put him to the test.

Immediately after the Job disaster, God had worried that Satan would feel "empowered" by his victory—that he would start to challenge him, or even try to take over. But it hadn't happened. Satan had been very quiet, in fact. He had gone back to hell-building and God had barely heard a word from him since. All those worries for nothing! Satan had no real power, he was God's employee. The idea that he was, in any sense, a threat had turned out to be completely unfounded. Satan was God's servant and nothing more. So when God needed someone to test his boy and make sure he was made of the right stuff, he wasn't uncomfortable in the least contacting Satan.

"I need you to do another job for me," God said the next time they met. (Hell was nearly complete and they were discussing some finishing touches. How hot would it be? *Roasting.* How cruel would the demons be? *Merciless.* How long would the agony last? *Forever.* Hell was beautiful, God thought—a gorgeous little world devoted solely to punishment. God adored it, and his pleasure in it put him in a mellow mood.)

"I need you to test my son, Satan, make sure he is up to the task I have given him."

"How do you want me to test him?"

"Oh, I don't know, Satan. I'll leave that to you, you're good at that kind of thing, I hear." God loved how airily superior he sounded.

"Shall I torture him?"

"This is my *son* we're talking about, Satan. I don't want you to torture him."

"I'll leave that to you then."

God's lips curled. What did *that* mean? He instantly remembered why he disliked Satan so much; he was petty, mean, *small.* But no matter. God was not going to lower himself to his level. "*Tempt* him, Satan. You can do that, can't you?"

"I can."

"Good. Then—go do it, devil!" God made a casual little "scat cat" gesture with his hands, which felt lovely. His disrespect for Satan would have been obvious to any angels who happened to be watching (and there were always angels watching when he and Satan were together, God knew that), and he enjoyed that. Angels turned and watched Satan as he walked away, which irked God a tiny bit, but not much. Fine, the guy had "charisma" (whatever that meant), but he had no real *power.*

God and some of his favorite angels watched, eating grilled meat and drinking wine, as the temptation began.

Almost instantly, God felt his stomach tighten. Satan wasn't tempting Jesus, he was doubting him. Satan *knew* Jesus was God's son, *obviously,* so why was he questioning that? "If you're really the son of God," Satan said ("*IF HE IS?!*" God literally shouted, spitting out a bit of grilled lamb as he did), "why don't you turn those rocks into bread?" (Matt. 4:3) This was idiotic! Of course Jesus could turn the rocks into bread if he wanted to, but why should he? He had nothing to prove to Satan!!

Jesus' response was, honestly, weird. "Man does not live on bread alone. He lives on God's words." (Matt. 4:4) The second part was excellent, but the first part? God had no idea what it even *meant.* "He should have yelled 'HOW DARE YOU, I WILL DESTROY YOU,' that's what *I* would have done," God fumed. He felt unsure for a moment: Is Jesus up to saving the world? But then God saw something that warmed his mighty heart. Satan looked rattled. Jesus' response to his question had obviously taken him by surprise. Satan obviously had no idea how to respond. He looked at Jesus like, "Wait, did that even make sense?" For the first time that God could remember, Satan looked unsure. Was he being tricked? Was he being made a fool of? And the more Jesus simply stared implacably back at him, the more unsure the devil looked. God started to smile, then laugh. "Good one, Jesus!" he called out and instantly all the angels started chattering excitedly in agreement, "Good one, Jesus, good one!!" It was quite an exciting moment.

The temptation entered phase two. Satan took Jesus to Jerusalem and they stood on a high parapet, looking down. "Push him off, Jesus!" one angel cheered, but was quickly hushed as Satan spoke again. He seemed to have recovered his composure; he spoke calmly, quietly: "If you're the son of God, why don't you jump? Won't angels hold you up?" (Matt. 4:6) God shook his head, *extremely* irritated by this. "You're supposed to tempt him, dummy! Not continue to ask him ridiculous questions!" "Ridiculous ridiculous ridiculous" filled the air.

God did not like the way Satan was doing his job. It was disobedient and disrespectful; he'd been given specific directions, which he was *not* following. Still, the first time Satan had challenged Jesus, God's boy had clearly won the exchange. God waited for another odd, offbeat comeback. But this time all Jesus came up with was, "Don't test me," (Matt. 4:7) as if he was ready to jump off the ledge, fly around, then come back and punch Satan in the nose. The angels, waiting to cheer, made a few small "yays," but not many. Had Satan won that little exchange? God wasn't sure, but he thought it was possible.

Satan now took Jesus to a high mountain ("How did they even get there?" God demanded. "Did they ride donkeys?") and finally, finally, "tempted" him. But the temptation he offered made God's back go up: "If you work for me," he said, "you can rule the whole world." (Matt. 4:9) Which was insane! Satan couldn't offer Jesus that kind of power, it wasn't his to offer! This was a terrible temptation. Satan was supposed to tempt Jesus with *real* things, *tempting* things: Grilled meats . . . incense . . . pomegranate-colored fabric . . . gold balls! *Not* with absurd oversized claims that he couldn't possibly deliver on and which Jesus would have no interest in anyway!

God hoped Jesus would deliver a devastating comeback to Satan and put him in his place—or at least say something cryptic and hard to understand, like he had the first time. But Jesus didn't deliver a knockout punch. In fact, he just stood there for a moment, looking at Satan with those inscrutable eyes of his, saying nothing. "Why is he hesitating—why is he hesitating?" God demanded, his stomach tightening with every second that passed. *Was* Jesus tempted? Satan was good at temptation—that's why God gave him this job—maybe he was *too* good—what if Jesus said yes?

Jesus closed his eyes, took a deep breath. God held his own breath. The moment hung there for a moment. Finally, Jesus looked at Satan and said "out of my sight"—and God exhaled. (Matt. 4:10) The temptations were over. "That's the *last* time I ever give Satan an important job," God announced loudly. He then sent some angels down to tend to Jesus (Matt. 4:11), who was so hungry that he ate much too fast and puked violently—which, unfairly or not, irritated God.

Chapter Twenty-three

As God watched Jesus begin to play out his destiny, he was often baffled by the boy. "I don't understand his stories," he told several angels. It was obvious that neither Jesus' followers, nor even his own family, really understood him either. "Even his own mother, whom I *impregnated*, doesn't seem to believe in him!" God stammered. "How can that be?" (Mar. 3:31–33, 6:4; Lu. 14:26) For the most part, people looked befuddled by Jesus, and God thought he knew why. The boy was strange. There was something enigmatic about him—something vaguely unsettling. He was brilliant at times, poetic and insightful—then vague and obscure the next moment, then downright rude to his followers the next. (Matt. 15:16, 17:17) He sometimes didn't even seem to know who he was! "Is he saying that he already *is* the Son of Man or that he's going to *return* as the Son of Man?" God demanded, more than once. (Matt. 25:31 vs. 26:2)

Some of what Jesus said, God found himself nodding along with vigorously. "Hate yourselves" (Jo. 12:25); "Hate your children" (Lu. 14:25); "You're worthless and will burn." (Matt. 13:48) Things like that were excellent. Other times, however, God felt that Jesus talked way too much about *himself*: Who he was, what he was doing, what was going to happen to him, etc. "He's very self-involved, isn't he?" God found himself asking an angel on more than one occasion.

And Jesus' magical powers? God was completely baffled by the way he used them. He'd given Jesus the ability to walk on water because, well—why not? He was asking a lot of the boy, why not let him have some fun? Also, just in case anyone doubted who Jesus was, walking on water seemed pretty convincing. But the way Jesus did it baffled God. "Why doesn't he walk around the sea on a hot day?" God thought. "Why is he out there walking around a lake by himself at *night*?! What a weird thing to do!" No wonder his followers thought he was a ghost! (Mar. 6:48) As for the story that Jesus supposedly kissed a man? (Mar. 7:33) Well, that *better* not be true!

The way Jesus administered punishment was deeply puzzling to God too. "I *believe* in punishment, I think that goes without saying. But isn't it important that it be, you know, justified?" God asked some angels. The killing of the fig tree just didn't make any sense to God. "The tree was out of season. Of *course* it was bare of fruit. Why did Jesus kill it?" God wondered. (Mar. 11:14–22) And Jesus' explanation, "If you have faith in God, you will do the same," didn't clarify things much. (Matt. 25:21) (As for the whole "eat this bread, it's my body, drink this wine, it's my blood" thing? In a word: Creepy.)

God began to grow annoyed by the way people fell all over themselves about Jesus' every word. He disliked intensely the way people seemed to see Jesus as his equal. They seemed amazed that Jesus brought *one guy* back from the dead. (Jo. 11:44) "I stopped the *sun* and no one even seemed to notice." (God had begun to wonder if there was some sort of conspiracy that kept his sun-stopping out of the history books.) God couldn't deny it anymore, and he didn't feel the need to: Being in the background had gotten old. He was ready to reassert himself with mankind.

"Jesus has had enough time," he proclaimed one day. "It's time for him to be tortured and killed." As for the mistaken idea that Satan had somehow played a role in all this, that he had somehow "possessed" Judas and thus *made* him turn Jesus in (Lu.

22:3)—this was *absurd*! "I was solely responsible for Jesus' being tortured and killed, *me*!" God fumed.

But was there a misunderstanding between God and Jesus? At a rather inopportune moment—as Jesus was dying on the cross—God began to worry that maybe there had been. "Why have you forsaken me?" Jesus asked him (Matt. 27:46), and this bothered God a lot. "*Forsaken* him?" he said in an overly loud voice. "What is he talking about? We had this whole thing planned from the start!"

Since God and Jesus had never actually met and had communicated mainly through prayers, visions, and dreams—well, maybe dying painfully was a surprise to Jesus. God comforted himself with the thought that Jesus would only be "dead" for about five minutes anyway. After that, he would travel to hell and try to convert everyone there. ("Not gonna happen," God grinned.) Then he would return to earth for a short time before he flew up to live in heaven.

Still, God felt he should do something to convey his unhappiness about his son being tortured and killed—even if it *was* his plan. He decided to send a massive earthquake, which he felt made his point extremely well. The earthquake was so powerful that graves opened up and some dead men climbed out and walked around town, which God wasn't completely sure he had intended, but was basically comfortable with. (Matt. 27:52–53)

Thinking back, God swore that he hadn't *meant* to leave Jesus on earth for more than a day or two after his return from the dead. What would be the *point*? Did God feel bad that he'd gotten so caught up in putting the finishing touches on heaven that he had forgotten about Jesus for a while? Definitely! As soon as he remembered, he whisked Jesus up to heaven. When Jesus arrived it was . . . well, why deny it? It was an awkward first meeting. God wanted to hug his son, but they just sort of . . . missed. God opened his arms, but Jesus first hung back (was he mad?), then started to lean forward—before God pulled back.

They never touched each other.

Still, you know . . . it was fine. Jesus told God that he wasn't mad or anything—that he'd filled the time by dressing up in costumes, then sneaking up on his followers and pretending to be someone else (Lu. 24:16, Jo. 21:9–13), which he found amusing. Also, he found that he liked to cook. (Jo. 21:12) The one person Jesus really did not like was a guy named Thomas, who'd demanded to be allowed to stick his fingers into Jesus' wounds. (Jo. 20:25) God found this repulsive and agreed to send Thomas to hell.

Jesus had told people fairly explicitly that Judgment Day was going to come very soon, within one hundred years at the most. He'd more or less guaranteed that, in fact. (Mark 9:1) Wouldn't it make him look just slightly less believable if Judgment Day *didn't* happen when he said? If it didn't happen, in fact, for two thousand years? Yes, it sure would, and God felt bad about that too. But listen—if God needed that much time to perfect the ending of his story, well then, so be it. And if that made Jesus look like he was a little bit "out of the loop," well, he had overstepped his place, that's all. Regardless of what Jesus or his followers might have thought, there was one guy in charge here, God.

Chapter Twenty-four

A quick aside regarding God's main messengers during this time: They were, he felt, a mixed bag. The first three, Matthew, Mark and Luke, were satisfactory, even if they didn't always agree with each other, even about, shall we say, important details ("Like me being Jesus' father, for instance!") (Mar. Chap. 1) But the last gospel writer, John? God had a real problem with him. First off, he seemed to hate God's own chosen people, the Jews! He even tried to make it sound like Jesus hated the Jews. (Jo. 18:36) "Jesus didn't say 'save me from the Jews,' Jesus *is* a Jew!" God boomed, irritated by this. Second, John made the story of Jesus' return from the dead sound completely ridiculous. He wrote it as if Jesus was stuck back on earth for—well, who knows how long, *weeks*! (Jo. 20:26, 21:1) Like he was so bored that he just wandered around "like a guy stuck at Spokane Airport!" God much later barked.

What *really* bothered God about John, though, was his self-importance. "He acts like he's the main character in the story!" God thundered. "He actually has the gall to call himself 'the disciple that Jesus loved.' He turns the climax of Jesus' life into a love triangle that revolves around *him*! 'Jesus loves me and wants me around and the other disciples are sooo jealous of me, but Jesus doesn't even *care* because he loves me so much.' It's junior high—*gay* junior high!" God growled. (Jo. 21:20–24) And that ending of his! "Jesus did lots of other things too"? Lame!

After John came Paul (actually, Paul came first, but never mind), and Paul was a *whole* different story. God liked Paul a lot. He liked how well Paul understood mankind. They were "wicked, futile, foolish, vile, degraded, shameful, indecent, depraved, greedy, villainous, malicious, treacherous, blasphemous, insolent, arrogant, boastful creatures," and Paul told them so, before adding, "But we have no right to judge"—which was also true! (Rom. 1:29–2:3)

God also liked Paul's language. Living correctly (i.e., saying nothing negative, only good and helpful things; having no bad feelings, such as anger or resentment; being nice and good all the time—not even discussing sex), Paul described as "wearing the belt of truth, the breastplate of integrity, and the shoes of peace." (Ephes. 6:14–15) "I could not have said it better myself!" God beamed.

Lastly, God appreciated Paul's feistiness. "He's a fierce fellow!" God pronounced, admiring in particular how Paul handled the circumcision issue. Some Jews were mad at Paul for changing the rules about circumcision. It *had* been important, yes, very. ("I did nearly kill Moses about it," God admitted to himself.) But it *wasn't* important now. All that mattered now was believing in Jesus (Full disclosure: God didn't like that too much; he was getting damned impatient to reenter his, yes, *his* story). When the Jews complained ("I chopped part of my penis off and now you say it doesn't even matter?"), Paul was ready. His comeback was priceless: "Why don't you go all the way and make eunuchs of yourselves?" (Gal. 5:12) God slapped his thigh with delight when he heard that. "Good one, Paul!" he cheered.

One event that really incensed God was when Paul went to Athens and talked to some so-called philosophers, who then laughed at him and told him to go away. (Ac. 17:32) "Time will show that Greek philosophers know *nothing*!" God muttered darkly to the angel who was massaging his shoulders.

A few hundred years before, there was another man who

God really didn't like. His name was Ezra, and although not everyone accepted his words, some people did. Ezra asked extremely impertinent questions. When God sent an angel down to talk to him, Ezra grilled the angel. "Your story doesn't make sense," he said. "All those other people who are supposed to be doing so badly because God hates them? Well, they're doing better than us and have been for quite a while, so how do you explain *that*?" (Esd. 3:30)

The angel correctly instructed Ezra that he could not *possibly* understand God's ways with his limited intelligence (Esd. 4:1), but Ezra persisted. "I'm not asking about the heavens," he said. "I'm asking about the world we live in every day." (Esd. 4:22) The angel sort of panicked and blurted out that in times to come, 3–4-month-old fetuses would pop out of their mother's stomachs and dance around. (Esd. 6:21) Ezra still didn't back off. "Why didn't God just make Adam good?" he demanded. (Esd. 7:46) "Why is he so mad at us if we are made in his image?" (Esd. 8:35, 8:44) "No more questions!" barked the angel (Esd. 8:55), who got out of there pretty quickly, and got quite an earful from God when he got back to heaven. "Why did you ruin the surprise about the fetuses dancing around?" God scolded.

Chapter Twenty-five

Two thousand years passed. For some reason that God did not understand, Jesus *aged*. He now had white hair, wore a girdle, and had darkly tanned feet. (Rev. 1:15) "Why did he only tan his feet and not the rest of his body?" God asked some angels. "And why does he *brag* about them?" (Rev. 2:18) "Also: why does he have such a high-pitched, trumpety voice?" (Rev. 1:10) Things had not gotten better between God and Jesus. It was still tense—if anything, more so. God still didn't fully understand Jesus; he felt that Jesus was judging him at times, not fully supportive of his great plan for ending the story, "Operation Punish Mankind." "Not 'kind and compassionate' enough, I guess!" God would mutter to himself.

Heaven was complete now and it was magnificent. The huge throne, the rainbow, the torches, the ice rink (Rev. 4:3–6), the singing eyeball-monsters . . . it was all . . . perfection. When God had first described his eyeball-monsters to Jesus, his son had looked at him funny. "We'll have *four* of them," God had pronounced. "One that looks like a cow, one like a lion, one like an eagle, and one like a man! Also! They will have wings! Six wings!" (Rev. 4:6–7)

"The eagle will have wings too, Father?"

"Yes, yes, absolutely!"

"Six *more* wings on the eagle, Father, or six total?"

"Six more! Eight total! Also—I will cover them all with eyeballs!"

"Eye . . . ?"

"Eyeballs, Jesus, *eyeballs*! All over them, head to toe. I will even put eyeballs *inside* them!"

"In their stomachs, Father?"

"In their stomachs, their hearts, their kidneys, their bones, everywhere! These things will be overflowing with eyeballs!"

"What will these creatures do, Father?"

"They will sing in praise of me, Jesus! I have already composed a song for them to sing; it goes like this . . ." And with that, God began to sing. He had a good strong tenor voice. "*Holy holy holy is God, Lord of what is, was, and will be.*" (Rev. 6:8)

"It's beautiful, Lord," piped up several nearby elders who God had brought to heaven for their so-called wisdom, before he had realized that he didn't need their wisdom, he was God— at which time he put them to work groveling before him. "You are great, Lord. You made everything, *everything*," he had them say to him over and over again. (Rev. 4:10–11) It was not as good as the song, obviously, but it was still nice.

God could tell that "Tanfoot Jesus" had found his eyeball-monsters idea bizarre. But he had not wavered and now the eyeball monsters existed and did have wings and eyeballs inside them and it was *brilliant*. "They see my greatness even in their bowels," God cried to himself, thrilled. God loved his eyeball-monsters' fluttering wings. "They could fly if they weren't chained up near my throne," he chuckled. But they *were* chained up, and forever too, because their job was to sing to him *eternally*.

The eyeball-monsters did not all have equally great singing voices. The human-shaped one had a good voice, and the lion wasn't too bad, but the cow was often off-key, and the eagle was horribly screechy. The song did not sound quite as perfect as it should have—but it still sounded very good. And God adored the lyrics. And the way the eyeball-monsters *looked* at him with their hundreds of eyes . . . honestly, it never ever got old.

Overall, heaven was fantastic. Beautiful and elegant and classy. God looked forward to spending eternity there. But when Tanfoot Jesus looked around, he seemed unimpressed, disappointed even, as if he was thinking "You're the creator of the universe, Father, why do you have the taste of an effeminate dictator?" Tanfoot Jesus never actually *said* anything like this, it was more the look in his eyes, but God felt it, and it pissed him off. He began to think that he might need to create a new version of Jesus— maybe several new versions—maybe including an *animal* Jesus. He began to imagine a version of Jesus who would have a sword that popped out of his mouth and killed people! "That's the Jesus I should have created in the first place," God muttered to himself. Tanfoot Jesus was too old, too soft; also, his super-high-pitched voice invariably put God in a bad mood.

It was time to get started with the destruction of the earth. God rubbed his hands together. This was going to be *fun*. "Break out the seven seals," he whispered to Tanfoot Jesus. The first "alternate Jesus" to arrive was a lamb with seven horns and seven eyes. (Rev. 5:6) God was on a "seven" kick at this time. It had always been his favorite number, but he was kind of obsessed with it now. He liked three and a half too (Rev. 11:9); he was even looking for a spot to use one and three quarters. To be completely honest, the seven eyes didn't quite work; they were meant to look intimidating, like "he sees all"—but honestly, they looked weird. They all rolled in different directions and that made the lamb look brain-damaged. Lamb Jesus broke open the first seal and now yet another Jesus, riding a horse, arrived. (Rev. 6:2) "Welcome, Swordmouth Jesus," God murmured to himself. Swordmouth looked like a regular Jesus, but when one of the elders approached him with a garland of flowers—*ziiing*—his mouth opened and a sword shot out and, in a flash, there stood the elder's body with a blood-spouting neck and a gaping-mouthed head on the ground next to it. As the body slowly toppled over, God clapped his hands together in delight. "Ha*ha*!" he laughed. "I love it!"

The second seal was broken open and Satan emerged. (Rev. 6:4) Or, not Satan, exactly, but a very bad character who would be in league with Satan; he would be called the "anti-Christ." ("Kind of yet *another* Jesus when you think about it," God mused.)

God's original plan for Judgment Day had been simple: Go to earth, wipe out all the bad people (i.e., almost everyone) and reward the good people (i.e., almost no one). But as the moment of truth neared, God had begun to find that ending to the story a little bit . . . well, ordinary. This was the ending to *everything* after all and God wanted it to be bigger, more dramatic and exciting. That's why he decided to put an Anti-Jesus into the story to work against his team of Jesuses. (Wait . . . he *did* decide that, right? Satan didn't sneak into heaven and take over a few of the seals, did he? No—absurd.)

More seals were broken, three, four, and five. The third one seemed to release—who the hell was that guy? He talked like some sort of salesman. (Rev. 6:5–6) "Where did he come from?" God demanded, but no one really knew. Another seal split open and—*what the eff?* Why was Death here in heaven, riding a horse around, clacking his jaws and pointing a bony finger at people? (Rev. 6:8)

As the sixth seal broke open, God sent a bunch of stars crashing into earth. (Rev 6:13) (He was surprised in a way that they didn't destroy the earth. They were apparently very small stars, he concluded.) God then rolled the sky up like a scroll, which looked incredible. (Rev. 6:14) He smiled thinly and announced loudly to his angels, elders, and eyeball-monsters: "Now things are going to get really interesting!" Some angels blew their trumpets (which sounded irritatingly like Tanfoot Jesus' voice), the seventh seal was broken open and, in short order: God sent bloody rain ("Good thing I've been collecting blood for so long," he murmured approvingly to himself), burned up half the earth, sent giant flaming mountains crashing into the ocean, turned a third of the oceans to blood, and extinguished a third of the sun, moon, and stars. (Rev. 8:7–12) ("Wait . . . can I 'extinguish' the moon? It's a rock.")

By the time God was done doing all this, to assorted "ooohhs" and "aaahhhs" from his angels, earth was a charred, bloody mess. People were screaming in terror; it was wonderful. (His 144,000 followers on earth were also getting punished, but hey, you can't make an omelette without breaking some eggs now, can you? Something occurred to God: "After all this time, all the tens of billions of people who've walked the planet, after all my efforts, I only have *144,000* followers? Isn't that kind of an embarrassingly low number?" A moment later, he bellowed, "No, it is excellent!" to no one.) God hadn't let humans have it like this since . . . well, *ever*, really, but at least since the Flood. After that, he'd made that unfortunate promise to Noah not to kill everyone, and he had stuck to it . . . but damn, he had missed this. Humans had frustrated him for *thousands* of years, and now, finally, he was getting payback. "And in a delightfully eclectic variety of ways, if I do say so myself!" he crowed to his angels, who applauded him vigorously.

"And guess *what?*" God proclaimed over their applause: "You ain't seen nothin' yet!" God sent another star crashing into earth. This was not a regular star, however; *this* star was filled with insects that would sting his enemies for five straight months. (God later realized he should have made it either three and a half or seven months.) That was splendid, but the best thing about these insects was that they had little human faces and long hair and wore little *gold crowns!* (Rev. 9:7–8) "*Any* god could torment mankind with stinging insects!" God boasted to his angels. "Only *I* can send insects that have little faces and wear crowns!"

Heaven was still buzzing about the crowned, tiny-faced insects when God, riding a wave of creativity, topped himself by sending two million angels down to earth on horseback to attack the humans. "Why do angels need flying horses?" he briefly wondered. The answer came quickly: These were not mere flying horses. No, *these* horses had lion-heads and breathed fire! Also, their tails were snakes that bit people! (Rev. 9:17–19) There were gasps of amazement and wonder from the elders and angels as God created them. "BRAVO, LORD!" an elder cried out. So *what* if some of the lion-heads attacked some of the horse-bodies and mauled them midair, causing them to plummet to earth? It *looked* fantastic!

God sat back, basking in the adulation. This had been an incredible run for him—imaginative and inspired. He felt proud and pleased, and looked forward to seeing his human enemies, the nonbelievers, shriek in horror at his wrath, then renounce their beliefs and beg for his forgiveness. He would not give it to them, of course. It was far too late for that; they were going to suffer on earth before they suffered eternally in hell. But he did look forward to seeing them grovel. God loved to see people grovel, he made no apologies for that.

But those fucking humans were enraging to the bitter end. Even at *this* moment, when it could not possibly have been more obvious that God was punishing them for their disbelief—even now!—*unbelievable*—what was wrong with these fools?—they *still* didn't believe in him! (Rev. 9:20–21) No one pleaded for mercy or forgiveness. They just more or less ignored him. "Who do they think is *doing* all this?!" he thundered at his cowering elders. God found himself briefly discouraged by this turn of events. He sat and stared down at the devastated, smoking, blood-sticky earth and shook his head. "What do you people *want* from me?" he whispered to himself.

Looking to one side, God saw Tanfoot Jesus gazing at him with a strange expression on his face. What was it? Dismay? Revulsion? Pity? God stared back at Tanfoot until his son looked away. Suddenly there was a ruckus among the angels and elders looking down at earth.

Chapter Twenty-six

The Antichrist had emerged from hell and was now killing God's people. (Rev. 11:7) Enraged, God caused a huge earthquake. (Rev. 11:12) And at that moment, something utterly unexpected happened: For an instant, *everyone on earth loved and respected God!* (Rev. 11:13) He almost couldn't believe what he was seeing: "What did I just *do*?" he wondered. "I've caused hundreds of earthquakes, why did that one work?" He didn't know, but it was a glorious, albeit fleeting, moment. The elders threw themselves at his feet and proclaimed his greatness, which they did all the time, sure, but at that moment, it felt very good.

One of the elders looked up at God from the ground and encouraged him to destroy earth. (Rev. 11:18) God looked down at him, deeply irritated, thinking, "Have you been paying any attention, old man? I made stars crash into earth and turned the oceans to blood and sent stinging insects with human faces and crowns and you say to me, 'Destroy it!'" God was so annoyed by the remark that he stomped this elder to death.

Then . . . what was *happening*? Suddenly a pregnant woman—it was Mary, obviously—stood before God in heaven. (Rev. 12:2) A seven-headed dragon was there too; the dragon flung billions more stars into earth (Rev. 12:3–4) (which was proving to be surprisingly resilient!). The pregnant woman gave birth, then ran away. (Rev. 12:6) God grabbed the child and sat him on his lap; he was fairly sure this was yet another Jesus. But this was all head-spinningly strange, to be honest. What was the chronology here? Hadn't Jesus already lived and died? Why was there a baby him? And what was this seven-headed dragon doing in heaven? If it was Satan—God instantly knew that it was, who else could it be?—this was deeply unsettling. Satan was taking the shape of a giant dragon and entering his home?!

"*Was this my plan?*" God asked himself. And for the very first time, he knew that it wasn't. He worked in mysterious ways, yes, but being assaulted in heaven? No. Satan was not his servant anymore, that was evident. He'd apparently been biding his time, getting ready for the end of the world, and now he was attacking.

"Where is my *security*?" God bellowed, before remembering that he'd sent two million angels to earth to murder humans. (Rev. 8:15–16) There was no one left in heaven but the old men, the eyeball-monsters, Tanfoot Jesus, and Baby Jesus. God quickly recalled some angels to heaven and they sent the seven-headed dragon tumbling down to earth (Rev. 12:9), where he tried to kill the woman who'd given birth. God, looking down, Baby Jesus on his lap, was incensed. "How dare he try to kill the mother of my son!" he boomed. He handed Baby Jesus to Tanfoot Jesus, saying, "Here, he's you as a baby, take care of him."

God was pleased, though somewhat surprised, when the woman sprouted wings and flew away. (Rev. 12:14) Then his jaw dropped as he saw a beast emerge from the ocean. God had to admit that this beast was a pretty inspired creation. It was a lion-leopard-bear with seven heads. (Rev. 13:2) God even briefly considered whether Satan's monster was more impressive than his own flying horses, crowned insects, or singing, eyeball-covered monsters. He decided it was not—but it was damned good. ("It's like we're in a Godzilla movie," God noted approvingly to himself.) Satan's beast attacked God's followers and defeated them, which was infuriating, but what was even *more* upsetting was the response of all those vile nonbelievers. God had *hammered* them, remember, and they hadn't even *believed* in him. But now

Satan shows up and gets to work and guess what? Instantly everybody likes him. (Rev. 13:4)

Tanfoot Jesus tried to suggest that perhaps the nonbelievers liked Satan more because God had essentially made war on them, but God would have none of that. He was starting to loathe Tanfoot Jesus by this time. (As for Baby Jesus, he was cute, but he cried a lot and didn't sleep very well.) God was not happy with how things were going: Satan was "off the reservation," attacking him in heaven, then taking over earth and killing all God's followers and then, most infuriatingly of all, getting the love and respect that God had always wanted from mankind in the process! God knew how all this must have looked to his angels, so he loudly proclaimed, "Everything is going *exactly* according to my plan!" But he knew it wasn't true.

Most of mankind despised God and loved the beast. It was horrible. It was the worst possible thing God could have imagined, honestly: To be hated by most of his creations, while his enemy was loved. Satan was obviously feeling confident, because he now created yet *another* beast, and this one compelled humans to not simply love, but to worship the first beast. (Rev. 13:11–12) "He deluded them!" God shrieked when they did so—but he knew it wasn't true.

This was bad, this was awful. God knew he had to hit back, and quickly. He thought things over for a long moment, then literally gasped as a brilliant idea hit him. "I will stop Satan and his beasts by sending Lamb Jesus against them, along with an army of male virgins who all have my name tattooed on their foreheads! *That* will show them!" (Rev. 14:4) God clapped his hands together, extremely pleased with this idea. Satan, his two beasts, and pretty much the entire population of earth didn't stand a chance against God's lamb-led army of male virgins!

Or wait . . . *Was* this a good idea? Maybe he should soften earth up a little bit first?

Yes, that's what he would do. God sent his angels to fly around the earth with sickles and chop people to pieces. (Rev. 14:14–20)

It was extremely bloody and horrible—exactly as God wished. "I hate mankind," he murmured to himself as he watched people get beheaded, or lopped to pieces. "I always have hated them." He felt happy watching this dark and beautiful vengeance on these creatures who had hurt him so many times over the past several thousand years. "Proud of yourselves *now?*" he jeered as the blood flowed. "Disbelieve in me *now?!*" he howled as the heads rolled. God found himself laughing loudly, nearly uncontrollably, tears rolling down his face, his whole body shaking, struggling to breathe, gasping, wheezing with laughter—and for a second the thought "I'm like a crazy villain" flitted across his mind.

The only thing that would make this global massacre even more enjoyable was a song. God instructed some of his angels to sing to him as the carnage rolled over earth. "*You great and wonderful God, fair and true,*" they sang, while strumming harps. (Rev. 15:3–4) This was . . . sublime. Watching mankind get butchered while this song of praise was sung to him was one of the happiest moments in God's eternal existence.

Chapter Twenty-seven

It was irritating that even at this point, people still didn't believe in God, but you know what, whatever. God was past that. Most of mankind was hopeless. It was good that so many didn't believe in him, actually. More people to chop up and send plagues at! God turned the oceans to pure blood and made the sun explode. The earth was ravaged, brutalized, devastated—exactly as it had always deserved to be. (Rev. 16:1–12) God loved looking down at the misery and anguish of his long-time enemies, the nonbelievers.

Only one thing bothered him.

Where were Satan and his beasts? Why were they simply allowing God to attack them, and not raising a finger in self-defense? Was this another one of Satan's diabolical tricks? "I'm going to take them out," God suddenly decided. He'd had more than enough of Satan; it was time to remove him and his allies. God sent an angel flying over the beast's throne. The angel poured some holy wrath down and . . . strange, very strange . . . the beast surrendered. (Rev. 16:17)

"Why did he surrender?" God asked himself. Also: Where is the *other* beast? And, most importantly, where is *Satan*? Was this an ambush of some sort? God found himself chewing on a fingernail, nervous.

He finished earth off with yet another giant earthquake and

huge falling rocks, killing a lot more people (Rev. 16:18–21)—
but that was beside the point now. Satan was up to something,
and God knew what. "He's wanted to run this thing from the
beginning!" he thought to himself. "But there is *no way* I am
going to allow that to happen. Think of all the awful things Satan's
done, like . . . well, like talking to that woman in the garden! . . .
Or beating me in that bet about Job! . . . Or creating the two
beasts!" God was not going to put mankind in this guy's clutches.
"Absolutely not!" he murmured to himself as he watched his
angels finish butchering some children.

But how to handle Satan?—that was the question. He
couldn't just be "killed" for two reasons: (1) He seemed to be
immortal and eternal, like God, and (2) God *did* need him to
run hell. He wasn't happy about this, but it was how it was. Hell
had been Satan's idea, and he was the only one who could run it.
God thought the situation over for a long moment, then nodded
decisively. He knew exactly what to do.

The next day, God and Satan met in secret, in what had been
a lush forest on earth, but was now a scorched, bloody wasteland.
It was near dark.

Satan gazed coolly at God, hesitated for a moment, then said,
"So you're suggesting that we share power then?"

God shook his head firmly. "No, Satan, that is *not* what I
said," he instantly retorted. "What I am proposing is not a 'power
sharing agreement' in *any* sense. What I said was that *if* you help
me with punishing Babylon—"

"Wait, you're *still* hung up on Babylon?" (Rev. 16:19)

"I vowed to destroy it and I intend to."

"And sending 30 billion suns into the earth wasn't enough
punishment?"

"No, it was not, *Babylon is a whore.*" (Rev. 17:1) "Now will
you please let me finish?"

"Go on."

"*If* you help me with Babylon, then I will . . . ahem . . . assist
you."

"Meaning?"

"Meaning . . . In the final battle between us, which we both know is inevitable, you—*sometimes*—will be allowed to win."

"Uh huh."

"Also, when you lose and are imprisoned, it will be, shall we say . . . temporary."

"How temporary?"

"A million years."

"Much too long."

"Fine. A hundred thousand years then."

"No."

"Ten thousand, and I will *not* go lower, Satan."

"One thousand."

"*One thousand*?! No, absolutely not! That will fly by."

"Exactly."

There was a long silence; God and Satan stared at each other. God looked irate, Satan was impassive. Finally, he started to turn away. "Punish Babylon yourself, God."

God gritted his teeth, hesitated for a second, then called out: "Fine, a thousand years then! But *after* that, when you are released, Satan, understand that you will be flung into the lake of fire."

"By who?"

"By Jesus—one of them anyway. Not Tanfoot, he's a pussy."

"Why don't you kill me yourself, God?"

"Because I want one of my Jesuses to do it, *alright*?"

"Because you're scared of me and always have been is more like it."

God was aghast, disbelieving. "How dare—?"

"What kind of man sends his child to fight for him? *A coward, that's who.*"

"ENOUGH!"

Silence. Satan stared at God for a moment, then suddenly nodded. "Fine, it's a deal. We'll share power."

"I specifically *told* you—!"

Satan talked right over God. "Since you're obviously too weak to punish Babylon yourself, I'll do it for you. I'll let you imprison me for a thousand years, then go back to hell when your son quote unquote 'kills' me. I'll play dead there for awhile before I come back and we start this whole business all over again, as we have so many times before."

God gasped, shocked at Satan's insolence. "That is an absurd way to—!"

"Here's a contract. Sign right there."

"What, you drew up a contract?"

"That's right."

"But this was *my* idea."

They stared at each other in silence for a long, tense moment. Then God seized the pen from Satan's hand and signed the contract.

Chapter Twenty-eight

The secret deal was made and put into practice. Satan let Babylon have it, which was excellent. As angels watched Babylon destroyed, they yelled down, "Kill her, burn her!" (Rev. 17:16–17) God felt a little bit weird, because they were essentially cheering for Satan at that moment. But it was so gratifying to see that slutty whore Babylon destroyed that God couldn't help but join in the cheering: "Kill her, burn her, kill her, burn her!" Swordmouth Jesus got ready to swoop down to earth to battle Satan. His blood-red robe had "King of Kings, Lord of Lords" written on it. (Rev. 19:16) That showed confidence, God thought. (Or did it? Would Satan wear a hat that said "Prince of Darkness"? God wondered. Was there something vaguely desperate about it?)

Swordmouth Jesus looked great flying down to earth, fearsome and righteous. God looked forward to the battle that was about to take place between Swordmouth and Satan. Satan would lose the battle, that had already been agreed upon. He would then be locked up for the also-agreed-upon thousand years. God smiled eagerly, very much looking forward to this fight.

And then . . . what the hell *happened*? Did he fall asleep for a minute or something? One moment, Swordmouth Jesus was zooming down to earth, the next moment Satan's two beasts were being tossed into the lake of fire! (Rev. 19:20) God shook his head, confused. Had there been a climactic fight between the beasts and Swordmouth Jesus, which culminated in Jesus shooting his sword out of his mouth and causing the beasts to topple backwards into hell? God liked to think so, but he had no idea, and that was annoying. After all this time, Jesus and the beasts had had it out and he'd *missed it*?

Apparently what happened is that Jesus had killed all of Satan's followers with his mouth-sword and afterward had pitched the beasts into hell. Then after that, Satan and Swordmouth had faced off, ready to fight, but before they could, an angel had flown down, grabbed Satan and locked him up for the agreed-upon thousand years. (Rev 20:2) When Tanfoot Jesus saw this happening, he looked at God, confused. "We *had* him, Father. Why didn't you let that me kill him?" God shook his head, dismissive. "I have my reasons, Tanfoot Jesus."

"But you hate Satan, why didn't you let that other me finish him off?"

"You wouldn't understand, Tanfoot."

"What, did you make some sort of *deal* with him?"

"Do *not* ask such disrespectful questions, Tanfoot!"

"Is it because you need Satan? Because your whole creation is so much about *punishment* that you can't do without him?" Tanfoot said, in his high, trumpety voice.

"Silence, Tanfoot!!"

Baby Jesus, in Tanfoot's arms, was crying now, and glaring at God, as if he knew something. Which, of course, he didn't; he was a *baby*. The Elders and the eyeball-monsters had also noticed this flare-up and were looking at God and Tanfoot Jesus, uncertain.

"Are you so weak that you can't destroy Satan, Father, or are you so cruel that you choose to keep him around?"

God suddenly lunged at Tanfoot and grabbed him by the throat, starting to throttle him, exactly as he had throttled Moses so long before. Baby Jesus shrieked in terror and everyone else present looked on in shock as God started to squeeze the life out of his insubordinate son.

"How *dare* you doubt me, Tanfoot," God whispered harshly. "I never should have made you. I don't need you, I don't need *anybody*. All you do is doubt me, all anyone has *ever* done is doubt me and I'VE HAD ENOUGH, I'LL KILL YOU ALL, *EVERY LAST ONE OF YOU!*" Tanfoot's face turned red, he could barely speak, but he managed to croak out, "You're . . . evil." Suddenly God felt a hard slam in the back of his legs. His grip loosened, his knees half-buckled, and he wobbily spun around to see Lamb Jesus breathing heavily, crazy eyes glaring at him, nostrils flaring.

This was not good, God realized; he'd created too many Jesuses and they were starting to team up against him! Wincing in pain, God looked at the Lamb, then at Tanfoot and the Baby. Should I kill them all right now? Turn some sickle-wielding angels on them and chop them to bits? It was a good idea, but there was a problem. God now understood that there was a bit of a "design flaw" in his system: *Nothing stayed dead.* Sure, you could "kill" things, but because of heaven and hell, everyone basically continued to exist, so what you were *actually* doing when you killed someone was creating an eternal enemy. God had enough of *those* already. He didn't need to make a bunch of Jesuses his enemies.

God slowly got up, looked at the three Jesuses, took a deep breath. He carefully sat back down on his throne. "I have spoken," he intoned, hoping that his majestic tone would quickly rectify this embarrassing situation. "I really hate it when I blurt out the truth that way," God thought to himself.

Things calmed down for a while. A thousand years of peace and tranquility occurred under Swordmouth Jesus' rule. By the end of this epoch, it was the year 3016. God was frankly amazed at how many robot-followers he had. Was that a good thing? He wasn't sure. Most of the humans who now lived on other planets had drifted away from him, so he wiped them out with meteor showers. There were also by now known alien civilizations in contact with earth, but because they didn't believe in him either,

God wiped them out too. "Earth is the *only* place I've ever cared about!" he yelled to no one in particular.

Swordmouth Jesus had done an excellent job on earth, but God's relationships with the other three Jesuses—Lamb, Tanfoot, and Baby (who, for some reason, remained a baby)—deteriorated further. They didn't approve of his plan, that was obvious. God sometimes saw them all conferring, looking at him. He was going to have to deal with all these Jesuses somehow, before they mutinied, which he knew they would do eventually. Could he manage to somehow send them to hell? Even if he could, and he wasn't sure about that, was it a good idea? Did he really want to hand a bunch of Jesuses over to Satan as potential allies?

If only those poor misguided humans who believed in what they called "reincarnation" were right. He could then kill the rebellious Jesuses and make them come back as worms or jellyfish. Obviously, however, these people were wrong. There was no such thing as reincarnation. God found it amusing that so many humans had been so utterly and completely mistaken about how life worked. "But to hell with all of them! *Literally!*" God clapped his hands together in delight as he thought this. He had a wonderful sense of humor—witty and quick—and he knew it.

When Satan was released after his thousand-year imprisonment, he proceeded to take over the world yet *again*, which was—yes, fine, what had been agreed upon—but God was *not* happy with *how* it happened: He'd expected Satan to come out of hell and kill a lot of people and (temporarily!) defeat Swordmouth Jesus. That would have been fine. But when Satan emerged from hell—"looking amazingly refreshed," God fumed—instead of just killing and tormenting people, *he tricked them into loving him again.* Most of mankind, who had supposedly been so happy and content under Swordmouth Jesus' rule? Well, guess what, they pretty much instantaneously turned on him and ran back to Satan! (Rev. 20:7–8)

This was beyond infuriating to God. Swordmouth was his

good Jesus, the one he could count on. He'd done an outstanding job running earth for a thousand years (lots of beheadings!) and now people instantly threw him over for Satan?!

"Why would they overthrow Jesus?" God sputtered in rage. The burning hatred he felt for humans at that moment was overpowering. They were the most hideous, vile creatures he could even conceive of! "Made in my own image," his mind taunted.

A climactic battle loomed between Swordmouth and Satan, and this one was for *real*. Whoever won *this* fight was going to be the final winner of all time! God knew that Swordmouth would win, obviously, but still, given who he was dealing with, he didn't want to take any chances. He dumped a bunch of fire down on Satan's army and burned them all up. Swordmouth then grabbed Satan and tossed him into the lake of fire, where he would remain for all eternity. (Rev. 20:9)

And that was that.

Chapter Twenty-nine

It felt almost anticlimactic. After all these many thousands of years, the story was finally over. God had triumphed and Satan had been defeated. Now it was time to judge mankind, punish the wicked, and reward the good. Everyone who had ever died was brought back to life; the bad were tossed back into hell (where they had just been, sure, but now it was final). (Rev 20:12–15) As for the good, God had decided that he didn't actually want them in heaven with him, so he turned earth itself into a kind of heaven. He dried up the oceans (*finally!*) (Rev. 21:1) and created a very lavish capital city, New Jerusalem, which was bedecked in gold, crystal, and jewels (Rev. 21:11)—very gaudy and extravagant and fabulous, exactly as God liked it. The good were allowed to live there forever, always happy, never ill.

It was slightly disconcerting to God that even now, at the very end of the story, there were still foul, unclean people left on earth. (Rev. 21:27) What were *they* doing there? Why weren't they in hell, where they belonged? Why were perverts and wizards *still* surrounding heaven on earth? (Rev. 22:15) Why were bad things so damned difficult to eradicate? "Because they came from you, Father," Tanfoot Jesus would say; he was always saying bullshit like that by this time. "They are a part of you, and you cannot simply destroy them, you must learn to accept them."

God had decided to send Tanfoot Jesus to the moon. Lamb

Jesus he had decided to slaughter and eat, while Baby Jesus he had decided to use as a kind of "hostage" in the event that Swordmouth Jesus ever turned on him. (Which there was no hint of, by the way; Swordmouth was his "go-to" Jesus.)

In any case, Tanfoot was wrong. Evil persisted not because it was a manifestation of God's nature—that idea was, honestly, completely discredited by this time. Evil came, as it always had, from two places: (1) Satan, who had turned out to be much more powerful than God thought he was, and (2) Humans, who had turned out to be even *worse* than God had thought they were. ("And I thought they were pretty bad from the start!")

Like it or not, foul, impure things continued to exist on earth. It *did* annoy God, he would have preferred to wipe "bad" out—but it also made him extremely grateful that he hadn't allowed humans to come live in heaven. That would have been intolerable. To be completely honest, even "heaven on earth" was hard for God to stomach at times. He found himself wondering whether even the so-called good people who were living in New Jerusalem were all that good. Did they really love and respect him? Why should he assume they did when pretty much no one before them ever had?!

"I need to test them again, and I know *exactly* how to do it," God proclaimed.

"I will put a tree of life in the middle of their city, ha!" (Rev. 22:2) When Tanfoot heard about this, he shook his head sadly and said, "Why are you putting a tree of life where people are going to live forever anyway, Father?" God despised Tanfoot by this time. He barely even acknowledged the question, he simply said, "You wouldn't understand, junior" and pushed past him. ("Soon you will be living on the moon!" he wanted to say, but didn't.)

Looking down, God watched his followers in New Jerusalem worshipping him and he should have felt good, he knew that. He had demanded that they have "God" tattooed on their foreheads and they had and it looked marvelous. All they did was worship him all the time and that was splendid too. (Rev. 22:3–4) But certain things continued to weigh on God:

1. People were worshipping not only him, and while God was fine with ruthless, fearsome Swordmouth being worshipped, he was *not* happy to have Tanfoot, Lamb, and Baby Jesus worshipped as, more or less, his equals.

2. God couldn't help but worry a little bit about Satan. Why wouldn't he emerge from hell yet *again*? God knew he would, and this time he'd be leading a huge and vengeful army.

3. Even the so-called good humans in New Jerusalem? They'd all turn against him eventually, God knew it. There was something *bad* in humans and it was only a matter of time before even the good humans began to ask questions they shouldn't—do things they shouldn't—*think* things they shouldn't. "They'll probably cut down my tree of life," God muttered to himself. "Or start having huge homosexual orgies. My creatures are obsessed with cock and always have been."

4. Dealing with two and a half rebellious Jesuses was not going to be pleasant. They might even try to fight him, and they were formidable, especially that Lamb. In the end, God knew that he was fiercer and more ruthless, and he would kill them all . . . but it wouldn't necessarily be easy.

5. Even in God's beloved home, heaven, there were concerns. The sickle-wielding death angels now had nothing to do and were starting to lop each other to pieces. Even God's beloved eyeball-monsters weren't as endlessly pleasurable as he had anticipated they would be. "I thought flying eyeball monsters singing to me eternally would be wonderful, but it actually gets extremely annoying at times," he thought to himself. "Sometimes I wonder if I understand myself very well."

It bothered God a bit that even as he was concluding his magnificent communication with mankind (others in years to come would *claim* to be talking to him, but they would be afflicted with every kind of plague for these claims!) (Rev. 22:18), Jesus was *still* reassuring people that his words were "trustworthy and true." (Rev. 22:6) It made him sound so insecure, God thought. Why, of course his words were trustworthy and true, why would that even need to be *stated*? The very final words of his book pissed God off. "I am coming soon," Jesus announced. "Come, Lord Jesus," John replied. (Rev. 22:20)

And God thought to himself: "What about ME? *I'm* the one who's coming soon! Why do you people not understand that? After all this and you don't even mention me?" God got angrier and angrier the more he thought about it. "I am sick to death of this whole damned thing," he thought to himself. "Sick. To. Death."

Epilogue

Before long, it would all fall apart. God would destroy New Jerusalem. All humans would end up in hell.

God would kill the groveling, useless Elders, snapping their necks like twigs. He would kill all the Jesuses, even, sadly, Swordmouth, who he felt was a long-term threat. In time, God would even kill his beloved eyeball-monsters. The human-shaped one would be the last to go, staring pleadingly into its creator's eyes as the life was squeezed out of it.

God would be totally alone again.

He would wipe out earth, then wipe out everything in a fit of rage, destroying the moon, the stars, all of it—hating it all, wanting it all gone, *forever*.

Two things he would find he could not destroy: Water, dark and implacable, which somehow had flowed back into the darkness (almost as if it was not under his control), the sea monster Leviathan hidden in its depths, and hell, teeming with millions of souls who hated him, ruled by his arch-nemesis, Satan.

Disturbing.

God would sit in silence for a very long time, brooding, considering.

Then he would think of something.

He would try again.

This time it would be better, he was certain of it. *This* time his creations would love him. *This* time Satan would not be allowed to interfere. *This time it would all be different.*

Out of the darkness and stillness, God would speak.

"Let there be light."

POSTSCRIPT: SATAN'S STORY

One

I don't know where I came from. None of us do. Most of us don't claim to. Only the Old Man does that. He claims that he's been around forever and that he created everything, including me—and I can't rule it out absolutely—but I doubt it. The truth is, someone else might have made us both. Or we may never have been "made" at all; we may actually be "eternal."

Anyway, after what felt like an eternity of cold, empty silence, out of nowhere, everything started to suddenly *move*. Just as it began (or was it just *before*, I still don't honestly know), I heard the Old Man yell, "Let there be light!" As if *he* was doing it. Or maybe he *did* do it. A lot hinges on that moment, really—and there's no way for me to know for sure what happened. All I know is that in an instant, where there had been essentially nothingness, there was now . . . well, *something*.

The Old Man stood about 100 feet away from me, naked. As I studied him from the shadows (that first light was quite dim), he looked down at his body—then slowly began feeling himself. When he got to his penis, he stopped and stared down at it. He touched it and his eyes widened. Had he never done this before, I wondered? I'd been doing it since—well, as long as I could remember. But maybe he hadn't. He certainly *acted* like he hadn't. He looked shocked for a moment, then upset, even mad. He yanked his hand away and quickly covered himself with a white robe, then stood there in the faint light for a while. "Let there be sky!" he suddenly called out and once again, I'll be damned if it didn't happen. Was he making these things occur? I'd have to assume he was, yes. Especially after he called for "land" and suddenly, in the darkness below, there was an entire *planet*.

Now there was no sun yet, remember—no stars at all. The only illumination was from that dim first light the Old Man had called for—but now there was *a planet* below us. I didn't know much anything about—well, *anything* really at that time, but even so, I had a feeling that the Old Man was proceeding in a very misguided way here. It seemed obvious to me that *a star* should have come before a planet. ("It was at that moment that I first realized what an idiot we were dealing with here," Baal later informed me. Yes, he was there from the start too. So were Molech, Zeus, Odin, Krishna, and many others.)

But the Old Man was incapable of admitting a mistake. Rather than quickly creating a sun, he now started covering the earth with plants—all of which quickly withered and died because there was no light or warmth. As he watched all the trees dying and plants withering, the Old Man looked enraged. "As if it was the planet's fault it was dying," I remember thinking to myself.

I could tell from the whispered furor around me that the other gods were worried. A single dead, reeking planet in an otherwise empty void was *not* what we were here for. This situation had to be corrected, and quickly. The Old Man stood there, glaring downward at earth. He obviously had no idea what to do next. Then he reacted in shock as, slowly at first, then faster and faster until it became rather dizzying, the sky began to light up with stars—literally trillions of them. Where there had been only the dark, dying earth, there was now—well, an entire *universe*. The Old Man looked stunned for a moment, then suddenly called out, "Let there be MORE lights!"

Two

I still don't understand why the Old Man created women. Why not create a reality where there were only males, which he so obviously preferred? I'm not totally sure, but my belief is that God had a powerful "feminine" side that needed to be expressed. He was terribly uncomfortable with it—scared of being homosexual, I suppose, though why that scared him I still don't know. But the way the Old Man treated Eve was unkind. The poor creature had just been yanked into existence, fully formed, an adult, given no time to grow up, and was now facing her creator—who seemed to *dislike* her. How can I help her, I instantly wondered?

The Old Man had placed a tree he called the "tree of knowledge of good and evil" (he was pretentious that way) in the middle of the garden the humans lived in. He told the man, Adam, that if he ate of this tree, he'd instantly die. I was pretty sure that was bullshit, that the point of this tree wasn't "knowledge," the point was "*obedience*." And I told the woman so.

The Old Man's reaction to the humans' eating the fruit was fascinating. He turned white with rage and literally stomped down from heaven and around the garden, yelling at the humans, "Where are you?" (He loved to claim that he "knew everything," but stuff like this kind of gave him away.) The man and the woman, poor things, were resting in each other's arms when the Old Man found them. He stood there, hands on his hips, a hard, cold gleam in his eye. But underneath his anger I saw something else: a tiny little smile. The Old Man was happy about the way this had gone. He *liked* being mad at the humans, I suddenly understood; he *wanted* to blame and punish them. "You will WORK!" he shouted at Adam, and I wanted to point out, "He's *already* been working, it's a meaningless threat!" But I didn't. "You will suffer giving birth," he snarled at the woman. "Another meaningless threat," I wanted to say. "You were already going to have a hard time giving birth, Eve, for purely physiological reasons!"

But before I could speak, the Old Man turned on me. It was the first time he'd ever looked directly at me and it was.. strange. He looked imperious, utterly superior—but there was also a palpable undercurrent of insecurity in his eyes. "As for *you*, serpent," he said. "*You* will crawl on the ground!" I almost laughed. "Serpents *already* crawl on the ground," I thought to myself. The Old Man followed that up with, "I will also make sure that women hate snakes!" which was laughable too, because I was *possessing* a snake, I wasn't *actually* a snake. Why was he threatening all snakes? It would have made sense for him to say something like, "Henceforth, all humans will despise you, Satan!" But to issue empty threats to snake-kind? Weak.

As Adam and Eve exited the garden, the Old Man looked at me again and spoke, this time in a lower, quieter voice—less for effect. "Now that he's become like one of us," he said, nodding to Adam, "what if he should eat from the tree of life and live forever?" I stared back at him and thought to myself: "What the hell are you even *talking* about, Old Man? There is no tree of life. Why *would* there be? Who would it be *for*?" But here's the thing with the Old Man: once he said something, he would never, and I mean never, back down. He'd keep digging his feet in deeper and deeper to prove his original point.

In order to prove that there really *was* a tree of life to protect, the Old Man now created what appeared to be flying man-servants. They were muscular guys with wings dressed in short white robes, all of them quite handsome and athletic. The Old Man gave them swords and told them to chop off Adam's head if he tried to sneak back into the garden.

Three

With regard to that first family of human beings, I've often wondered to myself: What exactly did the Old Man *think* was going to happen? In order for mankind (the whole point of this thing for him, as far as I could tell) to continue, one of the two sons, Cain or Abel, would have to have sex with his own mother. Why the Old Man couldn't see this problem coming is beyond me. It seemed so obvious. For a moment, it seemed like the human story might end before it even began. Then I got an idea. I'd already made reptiles, frogs, lobsters, and many other things (all the things the Old Man doesn't take credit for, basically); why couldn't I make *people* too? So yeah—that's what I did. I made a whole tribe of people on the other side of the river. One of these people became Cain's wife and the populating of the world continued. Just like Adam and Eve were similar to their father (i.e., the Old Man) these *new* people were a lot like me: They were skeptical, doubtful—far less trusting and childlike. They asked more and better questions; they poked and prodded and picked at things. They certainly weren't inclined to believe the Old Man's story. I heard that drove him crazy, which I can't say I minded by this point.

Did it surprise me that the guy the Old Man picked to restart human life after the flood was a complete asshole? Nope, not in the least. The Old Man had awful judgement in people.

156

Of course he'd choose a drunken bully. Of course his "fresh start" wouldn't work any better than things had worked up to this point. Of course in a short time, the Old Man would be murdering thousands of people again. Humans were what they were. He'd done nothing to change their essential natures. He'd simply killed all of them off, then restarted, seeming to believe that this time everything would be different.

It was around this time that I met Baal for the first time. I can't say I liked the guy. He was shallow, tiring—extremely vain—and kind of in love with his own appearance and presumed sexiness to, he apparently thought, pretty much *everyone*.

Baal had a one-track mind. He was pretty much *only* interested in sex. It made him fairly interesting for a while—and then quite dull. But my people gravitated to Baal. They liked him, found him exciting. Which didn't surprise me. My people liked sex a lot; I hadn't told them not to. I hadn't told them much of anything, really. I'd simply created them and let them live. If they wanted to believe in Baal and participate in his ridiculous ceremonies, well, I didn't care—and as I said, I certainly wasn't surprised.

I *was* a bit surprised, however, when some of the *Old Man's* people were drawn to Baal too. The Old Man didn't know how to handle this. To see Baal, who was not supposed to even *exist*, attracting *his* people—well, it was priceless to behold.

I never got tired of watching the arrogant old fool squirm as he watched things happen that, from his standpoint, should have been "impossible."

A few hundred years later, for a variety of reasons—I think the Tower of Babel had something to do with it—I remember suddenly thinking: "This asshole will never be happy." I decided it would be fun take him down a notch. I'd just had enough of him, that's all. I thought long and hard about how

I wanted to do it. And then one day I woke up and I knew what to do.

Four

The Old Man was strolling around his heavenly garden with a group of angels, talking too loudly (as usual), gesticulating too broadly (as usual), and bragging (as always). "Job loves me SO much, it's incredible how much Job loves me! And did I tell you what a good man he is? He is *very* good. No, I would go so far as to say, he is *perfect!*" The angels stood there, nodding vaguely and smiling. "Don't they find him boring?" I often wondered. I later learned that most of them were, by human standards, mildly retarded. Good-looking, obedient, male, and dumb: the perfect companions for the Old Man. So no, I don't think they were bored. I think they found him quite interesting, in fact, poor things.

The Old Man hadn't done much work on heaven at this time; his giant remodel was still a few thousand years in the future, but you could already see what garish taste he had. At the center of the garden there was a huge, like hundred-foot-tall marble sculpture of the Old Man, one hand raised, the other on his hip, a stern look on his face. There were several "heroic" portraits of the Old Man hanging on trees. They were crude and obvious, like the work of untalented children. Turns out they'd been painted by angels. But the Old Man obviously loved them.

I thought there would be at least some sort of security around heaven. But no, there wasn't; I walked right in. When I was about twenty feet away from him, the Old Man stopped talking and noticed me. We looked right at each other as I walked up to the group and stopped a few feet away. There was silence for a moment. The Old Man looked puzzled by my presence—then displeased—and angry. Would he tell me to leave—would he *attack* me? I hoped not. He was bigger and stronger than me, and even if I was quicker and smarter (as of course I was, am, and always will be), he outweighed me by fifty pounds at least. But no, he just stood there, staring at me. I saw a number of things playing across the Old Man's face. (I'm good at psychology, by the way; it's one of my strengths.) He looked scornful, contemptuous, utterly superior. Yet at the very same time, he looked worried—even slightly *scared*. He wanted desperately to come across as "all-powerful," but he knew—somewhere deep inside him he *knew*—that it simply wasn't true. And the longer I stared back at him, the more uncertain he appeared.

Finally, he spoke with forced friendliness, as if to convey to his angels that yes, of course he'd invited Satan to heaven. "Where have you been?" he asked me. I quickly told him the truth; I had been wandering the earth. There was another pause. The Old Man cleared his throat. He didn't like silence, I could see that. Finally, he smiled broadly, thinking of something to say. "Did you see Job?" he asked me.

"He's a very good man who loves me." I lowered the boom on him. "Of course Job loves you," I said. "He has a nice life. Take that away from him and see what happens."

The Old Man's face instantly hardened. His lips got thin, white. Clearly restraining himself, he shrugged casually. "Go ahead and ruin his life then, Satan. You'll see," he said.

I have to admit that I was surprised when Job continued to love the Old Man even after I'd dismantled his life. I had assumed he would turn on the Old Man quickly. When I saw the Old Man the next day, I instantly noticed that he looked excited, ebullient even. He'd been publicly vindicated and he obviously felt wonderful about it. This time, as he saw me approaching, his face broke into a huge grin. "Turns out you were *wrong*, Satan. Job does still love me even though you got me to destroy his life for no reason at all!" he crowed, then suddenly stopped, apparently aware that what he'd just said sounded, you know, bad. It meant that the Old Man *knew* what he'd done was wrong; he'd just admitted it. The door was cracked for me, so I pushed it open.

"If Job still loves you," I said, "it's only because he's not in physical pain. Let me hurt him and then watch what happens." Would the Old Man go for this? He'd already told me before *not* to hurt Job, why would he approve of it now? He stared at me, obviously shocked by my audacity. His supreme loftiness slipped ever-so-briefly—then he forced a smile and said, "Fine, go ahead, just don't kill him." In less than an hour, Job, who was already grieving over his ten dead children, was rolling around on the ground in abject misery. This was the moment of truth, I knew. If Job stayed faithful to the Old Man now I'd be proven wrong and my whole plan would fail.

At first Job did stay true. I got nervous that the Old Man might end the wager at that moment, but for whatever reason— my guess is he was too busy gloating and preening in front of his angels—he didn't. And before long, as I'd predicted, Job began to turn on the Old Man. When he said God had "hedged him around," I smiled, knowing this would infuriate the Old Man. "*Hedged him around?*" I imagined him blustering. "*What does that even mean?!*" But I think he probably knew what it meant: that the wager was starting to slip away from him.

Five

I sent Job's friends into the story for two reasons, one small, the other large. The small reason was that I thought it would be amusing to have these three obviously awful men complimenting the Old Man and talking about how "perfect" he was; I figured the irony of that might bother the Old Man (turns out, I was right.) But the *bigger* reason I sent them in was that as these three jackasses kept hammering away at poor Job, he kept responding with nastier and nastier remarks about the Old Man: God was terrorizing him. He wanted to sue God, but knew he'd lose because God would cheat him. Then Job started challenging God to a fight and calling him a *coward* for not showing up!

A bit later, when the Old Man started screaming down from heaven . . . well, this was a glorious half-hour for me. To watch God making a complete fool of himself was pleasurable beyond words. Sometimes I closed my eyes and enjoyed the mad, irrational torrent of his words. Other times, I studied his face and body, relishing the rage and folly and fear I saw there. From the start, the Old Man's bizarre mix of overblown grandiosity and pathetic insecurity had seemed volatile. Now it seemed like it might actually explode. I couldn't *destroy* him, I knew that—but I might, at the very least, *diminish* him.

At one point, Job begged the Old Man for mercy, which I thought was grotesque. This poor man who'd had his life utterly ruined for no reason was now groveling about his own worthlessness? It seemed like what a child would say to a cruel parent to make the beating stop. The Old Man was beside himself now, clearly overcome with rage and frustration and wounded pride. Everything he said sounded either vaguely insane or incredibly stupid. He was breathing too fast, sucking in huge mouthfuls of air, appearing to hyperventilate. He looked like he'd lost his mind and gone over some sort of edge from which I honestly couldn't imagine him ever returning. I felt the sweetness of imminent victory. Where would the Old Man go after this spectacular failure? I had no idea, nor did I much care. He could wander around the moon for all I cared, babbling to himself about unicorns (which, yes, he seemed to actually believe in). Or hey, maybe he could die; gods *did* do that, I had now learned. Zeus died, for instance. He'd had enough, apparently, and so he allowed himself to essentially "not exist." Maybe the Old Man would do that.

I had gotten so caught up in the Old Man's meltdown that I stepped partially out from behind a tree to get a better view. The Old Man, looking paranoid, whipped his head around. He saw me standing there and suddenly he stopped yelling.

We looked at each other for a long moment and as we did, something became clear: the Old Man had made a complete fool of himself. My plan had worked better than I could have possibly imagined. But as we continued to stare at each other, it suddenly became clear that I had won nothing. That the Old Man would never give in, and that our battle—and yes, it obviously *was* that—would continue.

Six

Hundreds of years later, after the fall of Jerusalem ("Great judgment there with Nebuchadnezzar, God" I remember thinking to myself), I started hearing rumblings about his big new plan: the Old Man was apparently creating a son to "help him." Not to brag, but I knew as soon as I heard this plan that it'd never, *ever* work. The Old Man was a complete narcissist. The idea that he could play a supporting role in his own story? It was laughable.

What was Jesus like? Well, he was both similar to and different from his father. He was similar in the sense that he was strange and muddled in his thinking and sometimes mean as hell. He was different, however, in the sense that he was actually clever. I grasped that as soon as we started talking. "Are you *really* the son of God?" I asked him, partially wanting to tweak the Old Man, sure, but also honestly not sure who this young man was. I mean, okay, the Old Man said he was his son—but what did that even *mean?* "If you are the son of God," I asked Jesus, "why don't you turn those rocks into bread?" Jesus looked back at me with those inscrutable eyes of his. For a moment, I wasn't sure he'd heard me, and I was about to repeat myself when he said in a soft voice: "Man does not live on bread alone." I looked back at him, unsure what that even meant, but I won't lie—weirdly taken aback and, yes, impressed. The son wasn't a blockhead like the father. There was something subtle, even witty about his retort. The Old Man, asked the very same question, would have undoubtedly shouted out something like, "How DARE you ask me that, I will DESTROY you, Satan!!"

Jesus and I walked around Jerusalem for a little while, and then I tested him again. "If you really *are* the son of God," I repeated, "why don't you fly around a little?" His response this time was not as good. "Don't test me," he said, which sounded, quite honestly, like something the old idiot would have said. Jesus and I spent the next several days together hiking up a mountain. We brought a tent and food and water.

He didn't eat, even though I could tell he wanted to. It was an interesting few days. There was a lot of silence and some of it was quite tense. He knew who I was, obviously—knew that I was his "enemy." (Or *thought* he knew that anyway. The truth was, it was his Old Man who would soon be plotting his death, not me.) But there were other moments, when we stopped to admire the view or sat near a crackling fire at night, when we actually talked. The first night he wanted to hear about his father; he'd never met him, of course. When I told him what I knew, he got angry at me and said I was a liar. "It's all written down," I said.

The next night was different. We talked about the future. Neither of us was certain what was going to happen; we might very well have to fight each other—we knew that.

But at least for that one night, we hoped we wouldn't have to. We didn't hate each other, in my opinion; I won't say we *liked* each other, but we did not hate each other. We had a lot in common, really. I mean, if the Old Man did create me, as he's always claimed, then Jesus and I were sort of half-brothers. When I suggested this possibility, Jesus fell silent.

The next day, we reached the top of the mountain and looked out over the world. It was a beautiful day, cool and clear and bright. After a long moment, I spoke. "Work with me," I said quietly. "Work with me and rule the world." Jesus turned and looked straight at me. I think he knew what was coming.

Although it hadn't been made clear yet, I think he knew that tremendous pain and suffering and an early death awaited him. He *felt* it—and he didn't *want* it. Why wouldn't he at least consider the possibility of avoiding all that, of being able to live and yes, to rule the world too? Notice that I didn't say: "You must rule in *this* or *that* way, Jesus." He could have ruled the world however he wished, I didn't care.

Something flickered in his eyes. He took a slow, deep breath ... then turned and gazed out at the world. He *was* tempted, I could see it. (And remember: I have a *talent* for temptation. I know it when I see it.) He closed his eyes. He was going to open them and say yes and together we would defeat the Old Man and rule the world.

"Get out of my sight," Jesus said.

Seven

At that point, there was nothing for me to do but ready myself for the final battle that I knew was coming. By the year 2020, I had hundreds of thousands of well-trained demons, not to mention the majority of mankind, working for me. I also had something new: my own son, "the Beast." (I'd found a woman and impregnated her. The old-fashioned way, if you must know, and yes, I enjoyed it very much. I'm with Baal, sex is *great*.) My boy grew up and he was a natural leader, the greatest natural leader I'd ever seen; people *wanted* to follow him, they loved him.

The Old Man had become a queeny dictator by this time, a sort of depraved blend of Hitler and Liberace. It was time for me to take him on once and for all. The odds favored me, I thought. The Old Man had 144,000 followers, many of whom were male virgins. (Of *course* male virgins would be the Old Man's favorite people; of *course* he would think they were "pure." "Stunted losers," Baal called them, and I was inclined to agree with him.) Some of the Old Man's angels, however, had become fairly scary by this time. They were idiots, they always had been, but they had huge swords and they were good with them. They would be my biggest obstacle.

Or so I thought. Then came all those other Jesuses. Lamb Jesus wasn't especially impressive; no matter how many eyes it had, it was still a *lamb,* you know what I mean? Nor was Baby

Jesus, when he showed up, very worrisome either. But that Jesus with the sword that he shot out of his mouth?

Okay, now *that* guy was bad news. I can't tell you how many of my demons he killed with that sword-tongue of his. Imagine Jesus (because Swordmouth did look quite gentle and compassionate and "Jesus-y") suddenly shooting his tongue out like a frog and then having that tongue be a *sword*. It was terrifying.

The Old Man proceeded to fucking *hammer* earth. First, he sent bloody rain. Where he *got* all that blood I have no idea; I heard rumors of mass blood-drainings in heaven. After that, he burned half the earth. (He left Asia alone because it wasn't "his," apparently.) Then he caused mountains to crash into the ocean and, rather unbelievably, at least to me, turned the entire Atlantic Ocean into a giant pool of blood. (This was the Old Man's blood phase. He was obsessed with the stuff. "I want a literal—and I mean LITERAL—bloodbath!" he reportedly screamed to his angels on numerous occasions.)

This wasn't a "war" the Old Man was waging; it wasn't "justice" he was administering. No, this was pure, unadulterated *hatred*. He wanted to hurt humans, that was all. Like a sadist finally giving into his darkest desires, the Old Man kept topping himself in the cruelty department.

The little stinging insects with the crowns and long hair were frankly unnerving. They bothered people in part, I think, because they looked vaguely like the Old Man: angry little assholes with crowns yelling up at you before they stung you. I think they were supposed to be a bunch of little "hims" in a way—I think that was the meaning of their crowns, but I can't say for sure. (I can say that squashing them was exceedingly enjoyable.) The Old Man sent his half-crazed angels flying down to earth on horses to murder as many people as possible. Now why angels needed flying horses I have no idea. And why those flying horses had lion-heads—well, same thing. The lion-heads apparently kept attacking the horse bodies, many of which ended up plummeting to the ground and dying. The Old Man always wanted to impress too much, in my opinion. He was always less interested in what *worked* than in what he thought *looked* cool.

But here's something I had come to appreciate about humankind by this point: they weren't pushovers. They'd been around the block with the Old Man a few thousand times by now and they were not easily cowed by him anymore. Even after he did all that torture-porn stuff to them, a lot of them *still* didn't believe in him! If the Old Man hadn't gone completely insane by then, that would have done the trick.

Eight

While the Beast and his forces attacked the Old Man's virgin army, I decided to take the war directly to heaven. I took the shape of a seven-headed dragon and showed up in front of his palace. The Old Man looked enraged by my presence in heaven. "Guards," he screamed, "GUARDS!!" But there was no one there except those pathetic eyeball creatures and some old men. I breathed some fire at them and left.

On earth, the Beast now revealed his secret weapon: a giant robot in the shape of a lion-leopard-bear, with seven heads. (We all knew the Old Man's favorite number was seven, so it was fun to bug him by using it ourselves.) The Beast's robot was about a hundred feet tall and at first people weren't sure what to make of it, but then, as it began to fly around the globe, putting out huge fires, cleaning up bloody messes and crushing masses of crown-headed insects—well, people quickly fell in *love* with it. "The Beast's Beast," they nicknamed the robot. This must have shocked the Old Man. After all, what had he wanted from the start? *Love.* Who was getting that? Us. Who was despised? Him.

But then again, why *wouldn't* people have loved us? The Old Man had been torturing them for years while his annoying followers had scolded, "You're getting what you *deserve*." My son and I had stood up to the Old Man. We had a cool giant robot and we had killed a lot of those annoying followers—what's not to like? The Old Man apparently told anyone who would listen at this time that we were "deluding" people into following us, but that's nonsense. They just liked us better, that's all.

Nine

The Old Man and I met near dark in a burned-out forest near
what had been Seattle. I listened to him for awhile, then nodded,
getting it. "You're proposing that we share power then."

The Old Man bristled. Of course that's not what he was
proposing, no, not at all. What he was proposing was—well, it
was predictably insane. "Hold on," I remember saying. "We're
at war all over the world, I've proven to you that you're not
even safe in heaven—and what you're mainly concerned with is
destroying *Babylon*?"

"Babylon is a whore and I want to punish her."

"You're *still* mad about the Nebuchadnezzar episode?" I
asked, incredulous. "That was more than 2,500 years ago."

"I have *not* forgotten, Satan, now may I please *continue*?"

I stared at the Old Man, stunned even at this late moment by
the sheer strangeness of him.

"What I am proposing is this," he said. "If you help me
punish Babylon—"

"Wait—you need *my* help?"

The Old Man stopped and glared at me. "If you perform this
service for me, Satan, then I, ahem, will do something for you."

I stared at him, silent. After a moment, he continued. "As we
move forward, toward our inevitable final conflict, we will . . . "
He struggled with what followed. "How to say this? . . . we will

take turns winning." Then, quickly: "In the end, naturally, I must win."

"Why must you win?"

He stared at me, clearly confused. "Because I am God and my ultimate victory has been predestined from the start, Satan, did you not *know* that?" I was silent. *Did I know that?* "However," he quickly continued, "when you are captured and imprisoned, I will release you after, oh, let's say a million years."

I said nothing, still pondering what he had said. *Had* I known?

"A hundred thousand years then, but no less!" he said.

"One thousand," I found myself saying. He stared at me, hesitated—then nodded brusquely.

"Fine—a thousand years then. But understand this, Satan: your boy, the Beast—he will die in the end."

Something about that hit a nerve in me. "Why don't we fight right now, God?" I said.

"...What?"

"Why don't you fight me *yourself* for once?"

"I will not—"

"Who sends his son to fight and die for him? A coward, that's who."

"—Satan."

This was a moment I had not planned on. But now that it had arrived, I couldn't stop it. "You're not what you say you are, Old Man. You're not all-powerful and you're definitely not all-good. You're a scared, loveless, stunted fraud. This incredible world that we all made together—yes, all of us—and all you care about is whether people love you? What is wrong with you, God? What the hell is *wrong* with you?" And with that, I turned and walked away.

The end of the story (which, of course, is not the "end" at all) played out like this: after Swordmouth defeated and killed the Beast and his robot, I was about to kill him when—why did I let it happen?—an angel suddenly swooped down, picked me up and dumped me in a prison cell for that previously agreed-upon thousand years. I was told that Swordmouth was a harsh and tyrannical ruler. Apparently, mass beheadings (performed by him) were quite common. Swordmouth Jesus was despised by most people; they openly longed for my return. ("Imagine having Freddy Krueger as your ruler for a thousand years," I later heard from more than one person.)

Finally, in the year 3020, I was released from prison. In less than a week I took control of the world once again. Swordmouth had gone a little bit soft in the intervening one thousand years—he'd put on some weight and lost some of his quickness. He could be taken, I felt. We fought for the second time and I was just about to defeat him again when the Old Man, in a typical act of good sportsmanship, dumped a bunch of fire down on me from up in the sky. Swordmouth then grabbed me and tossed me into a fireplace and yelled, "Burn in the lake of fire for all eternity, Satan!" But as I descended to hell, I thought to myself, "You don't really *get* it, do you, boy?" This wasn't even *close* to over. I had almost defeated the Old Man.

The next time—or the time after that—or the next--I *would* defeat him. I had plenty of time. I had eternity.

About the Author

Chris Matheson is a screenwriter whose credits include *Bill & Ted's Excellent Adventure*, *Bill & Ted's Bogus Journey*, and *Rapture-Palooza*. He lives in Portland, Oregon.

f